"Need some help up there?"

Hearing an unfamiliar drawl, Lisa Sawyer steadied herself where she was perched trying to string Christmas lights. The staff of Ruthy's Place was in full-on holiday decorating mode. She wouldn't mind a little help.

Turning, she found a man standing behind her who reminded her of a Greek statue. Maybe it was the granite-hard contours of his face. Maybe it was his razor-sharp crew cut, or the almost clear blue of his eyes. Or maybe it was the way his stained gray T-shirt rippled over muscles that ran from his shoulders to the tops of his paint-spattered work boots.

Wow, was the first coherent word that popped into her head. Since she couldn't say that, she smiled. "Thank you—"

"Seth," he said quietly. "Seth Hansen."

"Oh, Ruthy's nephew. She said you were coming to help out with some maintenance and stuff." Reaching over, she held out her hand. "Lisa Sawyer."

Considering how strong his grip must be, she was amazed by how gentle his touch was.

Books by Mia Ross

Love Inspired

Hometown Family
Circle of Family
A Gift of Family

MIA ROSS

loves great stories. She enjoys reading about fascinating people, long-ago times and exotic places. But only for a little while, because her reality is pretty sweet. Married to her college sweetheart, she's the proud mom of two amazing kids, whose schedules keep her hopping. Busy as she is, she can't imagine trading her life for anyone else's—and she has a pretty good imagination. You can visit her online at www.miaross.com.

A Gift of Family

Mia Ross

Love Inspired

Recycling programs for this product may not exist in your area.

 LOVE INSPIRED BOOKS

ISBN-13: 978-0-373-08264-3

A GIFT OF FAMILY

www.LoveInspiredBooks.com

Printed in U.S.A.

Be strong and courageous.
—*Joshua* 1:9

For Ashley and Christopher—
the two best gifts I've ever gotten.

Chapter One

"Need some help up there?"

Hearing an unfamiliar drawl, Lisa Sawyer steadied herself against the bay window where she was perched trying to string Christmas lights. It was the Monday after Thanksgiving, and the staff of Ruthy's Place was in full-on holiday decorating mode. With the long cord in one hand and a dozen thumbtacks in the other, she wouldn't mind a little help.

Turning, she found a man standing behind her who reminded her of a Greek statue she'd seen on the Travel Channel. Maybe it was the granite-hard contours of his face. Maybe it was his razor-sharp crew cut, or the almost clear blue of his eyes. Or maybe it was the way his stained gray T-shirt rippled over muscles that ran from his shoulders to the tops of his paint-spattered work boots. Instinct told her he hadn't bought his ratty jeans that way. The way they bagged on his tall, lean frame made them look as if they belonged to someone else.

Wow was the first coherent word that popped into her head. Since she couldn't say that without looking foolish, she smiled. "Thank you—"

"Seth," he said quietly. "Seth Hansen."

"Oh, Ruthy's nephew." Lisa filled in the blank with another, less impersonal, smile. "She said you were coming to help out with some maintenance in the diner and the apartments upstairs."

"That's me."

Reaching over, she held out her hand. "Lisa Sawyer."

Considering how strong his grip must be, she was amazed by how gentle his touch was. Careful, almost, as if he was afraid to hurt her. As the scent of fresh gingerbread wafted in from the kitchen, the ceiling speakers switched over to the opening chords of "All I Want for Christmas Is You." While she held up one end of the lights and Seth pegged in a thumbtack every six inches or so, Lisa sang along with the lyrics.

"You sing it better than she does," Lisa's helper complimented her as he pinned the last length of cord into place on the other side of the diner's glass-front door.

"Well, thank you."

"You're welcome."

The hard planes of his face creased into something like a grin, and he offered a hand to help her down. After she landed, they stood there looking at each other, and she realized he was waiting for her to say something.

"I was off this weekend, so I haven't seen you around," she said. "When did you get in?"

"Yesterday morning."

He didn't add anything more, and she

couldn't decide if he was shy or rude. Then again, he'd been a total gentleman helping her the way he had, so rude was off the list. That left shy, and she could work with that. "Then welcome to Harland. How are you enjoying it so far?"

"Lisa Jean Sawyer," Ruthy scolded as she came out of the kitchen with loaded platters for two of their early-bird dinner regulars. "Are you grilling my favorite nephew?"

"Just a little," Lisa answered with a laugh. "He doesn't seem to mind too much."

Looking slightly awkward, Seth didn't say he minded, but he didn't say he didn't, either. The guy was so laid-back, he made a turtle look like an Indy driver. At least she wouldn't have to worry about fending him off, Lisa mused. Although she couldn't imagine any woman with a brain rejecting whatever advances he wanted to make.

Eyeing Lisa like he wasn't quite sure what to make of her, he turned to his aunt. "Which idiot jammed the fry skimmer down your sink?"

"Oh," she confessed without blinking, "that was me."

Grimacing, he shook his head. "Can I ask what you were thinking?"

"I was thinking there was something stuck in the disposal, and I had to get it out," she retorted as she poured coffee for her customers. "I'm sure they'll have whatever parts you need at Harland Hardware. Just ask for Gus and tell him who you are."

The expression that flashed across Seth's tanned features had only one name: terror. His jaw was clenched so tight, Lisa knew it must hurt, and her heart went out to him. He was obviously former military of some kind, and she'd expect someone like that to have nerves of steel. Something horrible must have happened to make this imposing guy so jumpy.

Apparently, Ruthy noticed it, too. Putting down the coffeepot, she took one of Seth's hands in both of hers and gave him a bracing look.

"Tell him you're my nephew and you're working on a project for me," she clarified.

"He'll get you whatever you need and bill me for it."

Seth relaxed a bit and nodded. "Okay."

Reaching up, Ruthy pulled his head down to whisper something in his ear. Whatever she said must have been just what he needed to hear, because the tension left his face, and he grinned. He had a really nice smile, Lisa decided. She wondered what a girl would have to do to see it more often.

"So," he said with a little more confidence. "Where is this place?"

"Lisa's not busy right now," Ruthy replied casually. "She can go with you, introduce you to Gus."

They both glanced toward Lisa, and she smiled. "Sure. No problem."

Taking off her ruffly white apron, she draped it over the back of a chair and met Seth at the door. He glanced at the mistletoe kissing ball suspended overhead and shook his head again before opening the door for her. The silver jingle bells hanging from the knob alerted everyone in the diner that they were leaving.

Just as they were about to go, she heard the unmistakable sound of a camera shutter. Looking back, she saw Ruthy standing on the other side of the lunch counter, a digital camera in hand.

"What on earth are you doing?" Lisa demanded with a laugh.

"I always take a picture of the first couple under the mistletoe. Then I add it to the collage." Motioning to the frame beside the door, she added, "It's tradition."

Seth groaned. "We're not a couple."

"You're two people under the mistletoe," she argued.

"We just met, Aunt Ruth. We're not the kind of couple you're talking about."

"You could be."

When he glared at her, she gave up. "Fine. I'll delete it." Glancing down at the display, she sighed. "It's such a nice shot, though."

Four people sidled past them into the diner, with three more close behind. Lisa suspected that if she didn't do something, these two would argue so long the dining room would be overflowing by the time she got back to help.

"It's not a big deal, Ruthy. Just keep it."

She marched out, figuring Seth would follow quickly enough. He did, but out on the sidewalk, he looked down at Lisa and grumbled, "She jammed that disposal on purpose, didn't she?"

"Why would she do that?"

"My hunch is she wanted me to notice you. She invented a kitchen crisis to get me downstairs."

"I wasn't even in the kitchen," Lisa pointed out. "How could she know you'd see me out in the dining room?"

"Those swinging doors aren't that high. With you up in the window like that, I saw you right off."

"She's quite the matchmaker, so it sounds like something she'd do." Since he didn't seem seriously upset by his aunt's supposed meddling, Lisa laughed. "I can't imagine what she's thinking."

Being Lisa's godmother, Ruthy knew her better than most. Well enough to know this soft-spoken handyman was nothing like the brash, outgoing guys she enjoyed dating.

"Christmas lights and mistletoe," he replied grimly. "They make folks nuttier than usual."

"I think it's sweet, her wanting to set you up for the holidays. Of course, you should get to pick the girl," Lisa added to make it absolutely clear she wasn't even remotely interested in being his Christmas crush.

"I'm not real good at that," he confided quietly.

"Most guys aren't."

"She's just like my mom. They think I need somebody," he said, looking over Lisa's head as a tractor rumbled down Main Street.

"Do you?"

As soon as the words jumped from her mouth, she regretted them. It was none of her business if he needed someone. Or no one. Still, she couldn't help being curious about why he constantly avoided her eyes. She also couldn't shake the feeling that there was more to his hesitance than simple shyness.

After a long pause, he shrugged. "I've always done fine on my own."

"I like my independence, too," she rambled to avoid another awkward silence. "Being the youngest, everyone was always telling me what to do. The best part of being a grown-up is finally getting to do my own thing."

"Independence is different from being alone." With an appreciative glance, he added, "Something tells me you're not alone all that much."

Her intuition told her he was trying to say something without insulting her, and she wasn't sure she liked his tone. "I have company when I want it, if that's what you mean."

"I don't doubt that for a second."

Irritated now, she had to admit his comment about being alone was dead-on. She hated it but she couldn't imagine how this stranger had picked up on it so quickly. Both of them seemed uncomfortable with the subject, so she decided it was better to switch to a less personal topic. Seth wasn't big on conversation, which left her pretty much on her own.

"What are your plans for the holidays?" she asked.

"Home with my family. After that…" He shrugged as if it didn't matter to him one way or another.

Having grown up in Harland, the baby in a large, loving family, Lisa couldn't begin to understand his careless manner. But God wired everyone differently for a reason, and she never questioned His logic.

As they headed down Main Street, she noticed everyone had gotten into the spirit. Garlands and multicolored lights framed every window and door, and wreaths hung from the vintage streetlights. Up ahead, she heard a Santa bell ringing, followed by a hearty, "Ho! Ho! Ho! Merry Christmas!"

After a few blocks that felt much farther, they reached Harland Hardware. The brick building was like all the others in town, old but well kept, with a blue-and-white-striped awning shading the glass-front door. Red, green and silver garlands were draped everywhere, and a set of speakers was pumping some kind of shop tool Christmas song out to the sidewalk.

"Now I've heard it all," Lisa commented with a giggle. "Did you know drills and saws could even play 'Jingle Bells'?"

"Nope."

She'd finally had enough of his distant manner. "Seth, do you think I've been pleasant?"

"Yes."

"And you don't hate brunettes or waitresses on general principle?"

"Course not."

She gave him a chance to elaborate, but he didn't take it. No one had ever treated her so coolly, and she was done putting up with it. Glowering up at him, she demanded, "Then what is it about me that you don't like?"

"Nothing. Honest," he added, as if that would help.

"You could've fooled me."

* * *

Lisa huffed so hard, her bangs fluttered above her crystal-blue eyes. As she glared at him, Seth pitied any guy foolish enough to fall for her. Sweet as she appeared to be, behind that amazing smile was tempered steel. No man alive could possibly handle all that attitude.

Even though the top of her head barely reached his shoulder, she didn't seem the least bit intimidated by him. She also didn't seem inclined to end their pointless staring contest, so Seth broke it off.

Looking behind her, he was almost surprised to see the latest rechargeable power tools displayed in the store's large bay windows. A building like this seemed better suited to old-fashioned planes and handsaws. As he reached for the large brass handle on the door, his heart suddenly seized in his chest, and he could barely breathe.

Panic attack, he reminded himself, pulling away from the door to take a deep breath and give his nerves a chance to settle. Hard as he'd worked to get them under control, they still flared up when he found himself in unfamiliar territory. That was why he sometimes froze up when people talked to him. He'd made enough progress in his recovery to understand what caused the bizarre reaction. He just didn't know what to do about it.

A quick glance around showed him no one was paying any particular attention to him, which was a relief. Lisa's concerned look told him she'd noticed, though, and he forced himself to act as though nothing was wrong. To avoid her gaze, he looked into the other window, pretending to admire the latest in battery-powered drills.

The face reflected in the glass looked petrified, and he let out a disgusted sigh. It was a hardware store in a Podunk little town, run by a friend of Aunt Ruth's. Thinking of her gave Seth's confidence a much-needed boost. Honest errand or sham, she believed he could manage this, or she wouldn't have sent him. The last thing he wanted to do was disappoint her. Once his heart had settled into an uneasy trot, he reached for the handle again.

As he opened the door and stepped back for Lisa to go through, the bell overhead chimed in welcome.

"Is that Lisa Sawyer?" The gray-haired man behind the counter gaped in obvious disbelief. "Never thought I'd be seeing you in here, princess."

"My nickname," she muttered to Seth. "My big brothers think it's hysterical."

"Is it accurate?"

"What do you think?" she demanded in a haughty tone he thought matched her nickname pretty well.

"I think I'd rather not know."

"Smart man." As they reached the counter, she greeted the owner. "You should be nice to me, Gus. I brought you someone to talk shop with. Seth Hansen, Gus Williams. Seth is Ruth's nephew."

As the two men shook hands, Seth noticed the *Semper Fi* tattoo on Gus's forearm. Faded but still clear, he could tell it had been there a long time.

"I'm not much for tools and such," Lisa announced, wrinkling her cute little nose in distaste. "I'll be in the decorating section."

She went left, looking up at the aisle markers as she went. Gus chuckled and called out, "Head to your right, you'll find that stuff in the back."

With a melodramatic sigh, she changed direction and turned down an aisle advertising window treatments. Turning back to Gus, Seth was surprised to find the man smiling at him.

"Marines," he said proudly. "How 'bout you?"

Gus's quick assessment kicked his pulse up again, and Seth waited a beat to make sure he spoke normally. "How'd you know?"

"Son, it's written all over you."

Feeling awkward, Seth ran a hand over his crew cut. Maybe if he let his hair grow out, people wouldn't peg him quite so easily. Sure, and he could get an earring, too. His mother would love that.

"Oh, it ain't just the hair," Gus told him.

Leaning in, he added, "It'll get easier, I promise."

Inexplicably, Seth blurted out, "It's been almost two years."

"Some recover quicker'n others." Gus frowned. "Some come home but never quite make it back, if you know what I mean."

"Yeah, I do."

Seth had seen a few of them when he was in the hospital. Staring vacantly at nothing, muttering to themselves, imprisoned by memories that might never let them go. Watching them had been the motivation he'd needed to push himself hard every single day, even when his body had protested. With relentless determination, he'd whipped through his rehab in record time.

However difficult normal life was for him, it was a cakewalk compared to others.

"I pray for 'em every day," Gus confided. "Those poor souls need all the help they can get."

Seth was careful to keep his expression neutral. While he respected everyone's right to worship, his own faith in God had withered under the brutal desert sun. The horrible things he'd experienced had convinced him that if there was a divine presence watching over the earth, He was far from the compassionate, omnipotent being he'd learned about in Sunday school. *That* God would have ended all the wars and restored peace.

Since that had yet to happen, Seth figured the whole thing was nothing more than a nice story aimed at teaching people how they should behave. If the Golden Rule were the law of the land, the world would be a much better place.

Gus seemed to take Seth's silence for agreement, and he smiled. "If you ever want to jaw with a fellow soldier, I'm a real good listener."

While most people's sympathy made him stiffen up defensively, Seth understood that the old Marine empathized with what he was going through. He wondered if his aunt had sent him here hoping he and Gus would hit it off. Knowing her penchant for aiding folks in need, Seth certainly wouldn't put it past her.

Accepting help was tough for him, but he acknowledged the generous offer with what he hoped came across as a grateful smile. "Thanks."

"Anytime." Gus rubbed his hands together eagerly. "Now, what can I get for you?"

"Aunt Ruth jammed something in the disposal."

"Again? That woman sure is tough on her equipment." Chuckling, he lifted the hinged butcher block to step out from behind the counter. "My professional plumbing stuff's out back. Have a look around while I fetch it for you."

"Thanks."

Whistling along with the power tools' version of "Deck the Halls," Gus headed through a door sporting a sign that read No Customers—This Means You. While he waited, Seth cruised the well-stocked store. Neatly arranged shelves and hooks held everything from plumbing and electrical parts to livestock supplies. There was even a section of sturdy work clothes. Several versions of the denim shirt Gus wore hung on a rack beside jeans and steel-toed boots. The prices were reasonable, which told Seth the owner recognized how much money his customers had to work with and made sure they could afford to shop in his store.

"Browsing?" Lisa asked from behind him. When Seth turned, she laughed. "Please don't tell me you're seriously thinking of buying clothes here."

"Maybe."

"We have some nice stores in town," she went on. "Just wander up and down Main Street and you'll find pretty much everything you need."

Seth looked at the racks, then back at her. "Jeans, shirts, boots. What else is there?"

She groaned. "You sound like my brothers."

"Is that bad?"

"Mostly."

When she smiled, he realized she was

teasing him, and he felt himself loosen up a little. Apparently, she'd gotten past her earlier frustration with him. While he didn't do it on purpose, he knew his reticence made it impossible for strangers to warm up to him. He appreciated her cutting him some slack.

"They sound like my kinda guys." He put a little extra emotion into the comment so she'd know he wasn't a robot. He wasn't sure why that mattered to him, but it did.

"Oh, you'd love them," she assured him. "And my brother-in-law, too. Men's men, straight through every strand of their mulishly stubborn Y chromosomes."

Seth laughed. The way she rolled her eyes was so cute, he couldn't help it. The wattage on her smile actually increased, and he had a tough time paying attention to what she was saying to him.

"...actual shoes, shirts made of something besides denim, a sweater or two," she said, ticking them off on her fingers. "You know, things to wear when you're not working."

Seth couldn't recall the last time he'd chosen his own clothes. When he was younger, Mom took care of all that. Then he'd worn one type of uniform after another. Lately, it was Mom again, because he didn't have the inclination to do any more than reach into a drawer for something old and comfortable to wear.

Until today, he hadn't cared much whether they even fit or not. He wasn't sure why it mattered all of a sudden, and he decided it was best not to examine it too closely.

"I'll think about it," he said, steering her away from the clothing.

While his very entertaining companion chattered on about designer wallpaper borders, Seth hummed over the price of a new table saw. Not bad. Maybe he could barter some handyman help to Gus and get a discount. Then once he got settled somewhere, he could set up a carpentry shop and start making things again.

Appealing at first, the idea quickly turned Seth's stomach, and he sighed. Looking down at his hands, he flexed his left arm, testing the scar that ran along his chest and circled his shoulder. It still wasn't completely healed, but he knew he was lucky to have his arm. Thinking of that horrific injury always led him back to the afternoon that had changed his life forever. He'd done his job that day, and by all accounts their mission had been a success. But on a personal level, it had cost Seth far more than he could afford to pay.

Very firmly, he shut the door on those memories. He couldn't do anything about the past, and these days his future was on pretty shaky ground. So that left him with the present. Sometimes he felt stalled, as if his life had stopped moving forward. The trouble was, he had no clue how to get it going again.

He loved his parents, but their constant worry had become suffocating. When Aunt Ruth had asked for his help, he'd jumped at the chance to come to Harland. He was hoping a change of scenery would help him get his life back on track.

If that didn't work, he was out of ideas.

Chapter Two

When Lisa arrived at the diner for her shift the next day, lunch was in full swing. So were Seth's renovations. Trying to blot out the constant screech of his circular saw overhead, she bopped from table to table refilling drinks and making sure everyone had what they needed. Around noon, she helped Ruthy prepare standing orders for the contractor's crew that was rehabbing the Harland Courthouse, a quaint old building that had stood in the center of town since before the Civil War.

Then, because their busboy was up to his elbows in dishes, Lisa piled the cartons of food and drinks onto one of Ruthy's catering carts and rolled the whole shebang down the street. The twenty-dollar tip the guys insisted on giving her more than made up for the extra trouble.

As she strolled back into the diner, she realized the sawing had stopped. In its place she heard the sound of hammering, and she wondered if it was time to buy herself some earplugs.

"That boy just doesn't stop," Ruthy muttered, shaking her head. "He's been at it since eight this morning."

Having been raised on a farm, Lisa could appreciate anyone who put that much effort into something. Aggravating as her brothers were, she admired their willingness to work at a job until it was done. Whatever flaws he might have, Seth's devotion to his task earned him a healthy dose of respect from her.

"He should have something to eat." She ladled up some of Ruthy's famous Irish stew and dropped in a spoon. Setting the bowl on a small serving tray, she added a thick hunk of soda bread. "Does he like sweet tea?"

Ruthy's withering look told her that was a stupid question, and Lisa laughed as she poured him a glass of it. "I'll take it up to him. Be right back."

To her surprise, Ruthy stopped her with a hand on her arm. "Thank you, honey."

"It's just food."

The older woman looked confused, then gave her a sad smile. "That's not what I meant. I'm grateful to you for being nice to my boy."

Intrigued, Lisa asked, "What was he exactly? I mean, we see lots of veterans in here, but none like him. What happened to him?"

Ruthy didn't respond, and she tried again. "He was a Navy SEAL." Nothing. "Black ops. No, wait, he was a spy."

"I really can't tell you," her boss confided while she banded a stack of twenties for the deposit. "I don't know."

"But he was military. I could tell that as soon as I laid eyes on him."

Ruthy's eyes flicked up to her, then back to the money she was counting.

"Has he always been so frustrating?" Lisa asked, feeling a little frustrated herself.

Finally, her boss stopped fanning bills and looked directly at her. "Seth is a wonderful, caring man who's been through things you and I couldn't begin to comprehend."

Of course, Lisa thought with a mental forehead slap. Post-traumatic stress disorder. That explained his odd reactions to everyday occurrences, his hesitation with her when she was just trying to be friendly. He came across as cold and withdrawn because his emotions were literally frozen inside him.

"That's so sad. I don't know much about PTSD, but I could do some research online. Maybe if I understood it better, I could—"

"PTSD," Ruthy scoffed, which was very unlike her. "That's the least of his problems. Seth has lost his faith."

"In what?"

"Everything. Anyone he hasn't known

his entire life, and even some people he used to know well." Her voice had started to tremble, and she firmed her chin in an obvious attempt to keep back tears. "He thinks God deserted him."

Lisa couldn't imagine the closed-off handyman confiding that to anyone, not even his adoring aunt. "Seth told you that?"

Eyes glistening with sorrow, she nodded. "We were all together for Thanksgiving at my sister's house. He was so sulky, barely talking to anyone, looking mad at the world. I couldn't bear to see him that way, so I kept at him until we got down to the real problem."

Frowning, Lisa said, "I remember when Matt was like that. It was awful knowing my big brother was so lost."

"Lost," Ruthy repeated. "That's the word for Seth right now, but I'm not leaving it that way. I asked him to come here, hoping a new place would help him work through his troubles and get back to the way he used to be."

Lisa smiled. "Does Santa know about you?"

"You're distracting me." Waving her away, Ruthy turned the stack of money over to begin counting again. But her pleased expression revealed how she felt about the compliment. "And that food is getting cold."

"Yes, ma'am." Lisa took the tray and turned toward the steps. "I won't be long."

"Stay up there and see if you can get him to take a break. I don't want him wearing himself out," she added in a worried tone.

"What makes you think he'll listen to me?"

Ruthy laughed as if she'd just heard the world's funniest joke. "Oh, honey, there's not a man alive who wouldn't drop whatever he's doing to talk to you."

"Not Seth," Lisa grumbled. "He's immune to my charm."

As she headed upstairs, behind her she heard Ruthy mutter, "That's what you think."

Hearing light footsteps on the stairs, Seth expected it to be his aunt coming to check on him. When he glanced up from the oak plank he was measuring for a cut, he was shocked to see Lisa instead. Flustered by her unexpected visit, he stood up so fast he knocked his head on the sharp corner of the wall.

"Are you okay?" she asked, hurrying toward him.

"Yeah." Rubbing his head, he added, "Just a klutz."

While she looked up at him, he hoped she didn't think he was a complete moron. To his relief, she smiled. "You've been working really hard up here, so I thought you might be hungry. I left the tray on that table in the hall so the food wouldn't get sawdust in it."

He'd been so focused on what he was doing, he hadn't thought about food at all. The mention of it made his stomach rumble. "Actually, I'm starving."

"Then I guess it's a good thing I showed up when I did."

Was it good? He hadn't known her long, but he'd really enjoyed the brief time he'd spent with her. Lighthearted and chatty, she made him forget about everything but how much fun he had listening to her talk.

Then again, she probably had that effect on every guy within ten miles. Seth wished he could just relax and let things happen between them naturally, but he was painfully aware he couldn't let himself get too attached to anyone in particular. He'd come a long way, but he didn't think he was ready for a sassy handful like Lisa Sawyer. He knew for a fact she wasn't ready for him.

That left them at friends, he supposed. For someone who felt adrift in his own life, there were much worse places he could find himself.

"It's pretty dusty in here," he said. "You don't have a mask, so you should really stay out in the hallway."

"Okay."

After he'd closed the door behind them, she asked, "Should I get out of your hair, or would you like some company while you eat?"

In reply, he pulled up a wooden chair and brushed off the plaster dust that had accumulated while he was putting up Sheetrock in one of the rooms. When he motioned her to it, she smiled and sat down. "That new floor you're putting down in there looks nice."

"The old one was pretty beat-up," he agreed as he pulled up another chair and started in on his stew. Humming appreciation, he said, "Aunt Ruth's a great cook, but this has always been my favorite. Thanks for bringing it."

"There's plenty more if you want it. She always makes way too much."

"Then she takes the leftovers to that shelter in Kenwood," Seth added.

"That's our Ruthy," Lisa said fondly. "Feeding the world one mouth at a time."

After swallowing some sweet tea, Seth said, "You really love her, don't you?"

"Since I was a baby. She's my godmother, and she insists I picked her the first time she held me."

"She was a friend of your parents, then."

Lisa's nostalgic smile dipped into a frown, and she nodded. Seth felt awful for upsetting her, and he did something he never did. He asked a near-stranger a very personal question.

"Is something wrong?"

"No," she responded with a sigh. "My parents are both gone is all. Dad died a couple of years ago, and I miss him most at the holidays."

Seth had pegged Lisa at about his age, and twenty-eight was way too young to have lost both parents. His heart twisted with an emotion he hadn't felt in a long, long time: sympathy. "I'm sorry."

"Me, too." After a couple of seconds, she appeared to shake off the sadness and asked, "So, do you have any plans after you're done here?"

"Not really."

"But you're not staying in Harland?" When he shook his head, she laughed. "Yeah, me neither. It was great growing up here, but I know every nook and cranny of this place. I want to get out and see some of the world."

He managed a tight smile that he hoped

told her he had no desire to pursue the subject of exploring any part of the world other than where he was currently standing. Thankfully, she switched tracks.

"Your parents must be so proud of you, coming to help out like this," she said. "Not many people would drop what they were doing to take on this job all by themselves."

Scooping gravy from the bottom of his bowl, he shrugged. "No big deal."

"Seth, look at me."

He dragged his eyes up to meet hers, and she rewarded him with another of her beautiful smiles. So far, he'd noticed six different versions, each one as amazing as the others. Not that he was counting.

"You're a good guy, and what you're doing to help Ruthy is really nice. Don't sell yourself short."

Her words were like salve to a soul that had taken more than its share of beatings, and he couldn't help grinning. "Thanks."

"Anytime. Do you want some more?" she asked, pointing to the bowl he'd scraped clean with the soft bread.

"No, I'm good. Thanks, though."

Giving him a parting smile, she headed back downstairs. The scent of her perfume lingered where she'd been sitting, and he debated what fragrance it was. He wasn't much for gardening, so he settled on something flowery. It made him think of summertime when he was younger, when the biggest decision he had to make was where the fish would be biting that day. And which fishing hole attracted the prettiest girls for swimming.

Those were the days, he thought with a sigh, full of simple plans and even simpler pleasures. It was a shame he hadn't appreciated them more when he had the chance. Pushing the past into the rear of his mind where it belonged, he stood up and got back to work.

Wednesday afternoon, Seth caught up with Lisa while she was at the lunch counter, filling a long row of sugar shakers. "Are you busy?"

Pausing in midpour, she cocked an eyebrow at him. "Do I look busy?"

"Kinda."

"Trust me, I'm not. Go ahead."

"This morning at breakfast, Aunt Ruth told me she wants to change out all the drapes and bedding in the apartments I'm working on. Then she mentioned putting new trim and a feature wall in each one." He made a sour face. "I know Gus carries all that decorating stuff, but I'm no good at figuring out what goes together. I was hoping you could help me out."

Glancing up from her task, she smiled. "You don't trust Gus to be your interior designer?"

"Not a chance. After seeing his store, I'm guessing he's not any better at it than I am."

"Well, it's not like I'm doing anything important here." Taking off her ruffled apron, she went to the pass-through and yelled into the kitchen. "Taking my break!"

A muffled response came back, and she joined him on the far side of the counter. "I'm all yours."

Even though he knew the comment didn't mean anything special, he liked the way that sounded. As they left the diner, Seth noticed how men's heads turned when Lisa walked by. The attention didn't seem to faze her, though. She was either oblivious to it or immune. Since her sparkle struck him as being completely natural, his guess was the latter.

"Don't those garlands look nice?" she asked, pointing to workers suspended in two cherry pickers, stringing long boughs over Main Street. "They're going to put lanterns in the upswing parts. That'll be so pretty."

"Yeah, this place really goes all out for the holidays. You don't see that much anymore, with money being so tight."

"People donate the funds to make it happen," Lisa told him in a proud tone. "It's important, so we make sure it gets done."

"Gotta admire that." As he pulled open the door of Harland Hardware, they were greeted by a unique version of "Carol of the Bells."

"Are they banging on metal?" Lisa asked Gus, who was filling a rack with work gloves.

"Hammers on anvils," he replied with a grin. "That's the name of their band, too."

Laughing, she shook her head. "Where do you find these albums?"

"Santa brings 'em." Sliding the last pair of gloves in place, he asked, "What can I do for you two?"

Lisa didn't answer, and Seth realized she was letting him take the lead. After months of enduring people's well-intentioned coddling, he liked that she was allowing him to stand on his own. "Aunt Ruth wants some redecorating done in those apartments. Lisa's here to make sure I don't pick out anything stupid."

Laughing, she patted his arm. "Why don't you hang with Gus while I check out the new stock? When I find some things I think Ruthy will like, I'll holler."

"Works for me," Seth agreed quickly.

After she'd gone, Gus gave Seth a knowing look. "That girl likes taking care of you, doesn't she?"

Seth's first impulse was to deny it, but after a second thought he had to admit Gus might be right. Because he didn't want to consider it any further right now, he opted for an old military tactic. He turned the tables.

"Mind if I ask you something?" he asked as he followed Gus to the main counter.

"Sure. Might not get an answer, but fire away."

"What's going on with you and my aunt?"

Looking neither pleased nor angry, the old Marine studied him through narrowed eyes. "What makes you think there's anything going on?"

Seth knew he'd hit the nail squarely on the head, but he shrugged to keep things casual. "You're in the diner at least twice a day, and even if she's up to her ears in orders she always takes your table herself." Grinning, he added, "There's a huge mug behind the counter with your name on it."

"Those fancy teacups of hers are too small for me. I'm just saving her time by getting all my coffee at once."

"Uh-huh."

After a few seconds, Gus relented with a hearty laugh. "All right, you got me. I think the world of that woman, and she doesn't seem to mind me too much, either. Happy now?"

"I would be if you'd do something about it."

Seth knew he was pushing it, but his aunt had been a widow for more than twenty years. She never complained, but he hated thinking of her rattling around in her big, beautiful Victorian house all alone. He was pretty sure if his uncle Paul had the chance, he'd tell her the same thing.

"And what about you?" Gus challenged with a knowing look. "When are you gonna do something about Lisa Sawyer?"

Feeling as if he'd been ambushed, Seth tried to spit out the answer that should have come easily. He had no intention of doing anything about Lisa, but for some reason he couldn't form the words. What was wrong with him, anyway?

"Yeah, that's what I thought." Grinning,

Gus deftly changed the subject. "So what is it you two are looking for?"

"I'm not sure," Seth replied with a grimace. "Aunt Ruth wants something called 'feature walls' in these rooms, and Lisa thought wallpaper would look nice. I'm no good with that fancy stuff, so she's helping me out."

Lisa shouted for Seth, and he grinned. "There's my cue."

As he strolled past the counter, Gus called after him, "I've got shower curtains and bathroom googaws back there, too. Be sure to check those out."

In reply, Seth just groaned, and Gus's laughter followed him back into the decorator section of the store.

By the time they were finished at the hardware store, the storm that had been predicted all week was picking up steam. Lisa decided it would be smart to collect the bistro chairs and take them inside before they ended up down the street. There were twenty of them clustered around five tables, and she was fighting the wind every step of the way.

Fortunately, Seth pitched in, lifting two of the wrought-iron tables as if they were made of paper. With his help, the job went much quicker. She was holding the door open for him when a gust of wind roared down the sidewalk with the force of a runaway eighteen-wheeler. Behind it came a chilling rain, and Lisa was grateful when Seth lined himself up to shield her from the water coming in sideways under the awnings. Signs creaked overhead, and the trees lining the sidewalk were bent almost double trying to absorb the wind.

"Wow, this is really something!" she yelled over the noise.

"Almost done."

He sounded so calm, she glanced over at him. Despite the power of that swirling wind, he looked as though he was doing nothing tougher than wading through ankle-deep water at the beach. Light as she was, Lisa knew if he stepped aside, she'd be blown into the brick wall behind her.

Suddenly, there was a harsh crack as a streak of lightning touched down close by. The roar of thunder was immediate, and she found herself flattened against the wall she'd just been thinking about. She could feel Seth's heart thumping a measured, reassuring beat against her cheek, even though her own was racing along in sheer panic. After a few seconds, he pulled away, and she saw someone she'd never met before.

Alert and rigid, his hands braced on either side of her, he looked ready for a fight. As if that wasn't unsettling enough, his eyes had gone a breathtaking icy hue. As his expression mellowed, the color came back into them, and he looked her over with genuine concern. "Are you okay?"

"You mean other than the fact that you just scared me half to death?" More than a little rattled, she hoped she'd managed to sound more or less normal.

"Sorry. Reflex."

Nobody she knew had reflexes like that. Quick and violent, they gave her a terrifying glimpse into his past. It was a view she'd rather not have gotten.

"What did you think was going to happen?" she asked.

Before he could answer, she heard the ominous groan of a tree and looked over to the town square. She watched in horror as an ancient oak the size of a tanker truck crashed through the roof of the oldest church in Harland. Whipping out her cell phone, she dialed 911 with one hand and dragged Seth along with the other.

"Pastor Charles's car is in the parking lot," she explained as they ran toward the little white church. "He's probably in there."

Before she even finished speaking, Seth broke into a full-on gallop, leaving her far behind. By the time Lisa shouted their location to the county emergency operator and got to the chapel, he was yanking boards away from the ruined doorway.

"He's in there, all right," Seth ground out

between clenched teeth. "He heard me and called for help. Said the roof caved in on him and he can't move."

Sending up an urgent prayer for the pastor's safety, Lisa helped Seth clear a space just wide enough for them to get through. When they had one, he turned to her and gripped her shoulders in his scratched, bleeding hands.

"Lisa, I want you to wait in the parking lot for the EMTs."

"But—"

The look he gave her would have cowed the Devil himself, and for once in her life she went the meek route. Above their heads, one of the remaining roof trusses creaked and shifted, sending decades-old dust down on them.

"Be careful!" she cautioned as Seth slipped inside.

She peeked in behind him, watching him wade through pews and hymnals scattered everywhere, then duck under the enormous tree felled by the storm. Tossing aside beams as if they were Lincoln

Logs, he made his way to the front of the church.

As the wind's howling intensified, more debris rained down, and she lost sight of him. The idea of anything happening to this bewildering, courageous man terrified her more than anything had in her entire life.

"Seth?"

"Why are you still here?" he barked as the wail of a siren broke through the screeching wind.

"I wanted to make sure you're okay."

He muttered a few things that should never be said inside the walls of a church, then she heard the word "woman" tacked on the end. She gathered he was referring to her, and not in a nice way.

"I'm fine," he growled. "Go tell the EMTs to come in the back."

This time, she did as he asked. Lisa scrambled away from the door just before the jamb splintered overhead.

"Please, God," she murmured as she ran

to meet the ambulance. "We could use Your help down here."

Choking and squinting against the dust floating in the air, Seth pushed his way through the mess. Near the altar, he found an older man dressed in a gray suit pinned under a fallen rafter. Covered in splinters and dirt, somehow he managed to beam like the cherubs Seth had seen flying around the Sistine Chapel when he'd visited Rome years ago.

"Oh, praise the Lord! I wasn't sure anyone would hear me over the storm."

"Lisa Sawyer and I saw the roof go in," Seth explained.

Despite his own predicament, the trapped man frowned in concern. "She's not in here, too, is she?"

"No, she's safe. The ambulance just pulled in, and she's talking to the EMTs." Falling back on relentless training that had become instinct, Seth quickly assessed the situation. Hunkering down beside the frightened pastor, he asked, "Can you move at all?"

"A little."

Ideally, he'd have a couple of guys to help him shore up the pile so it wouldn't shift uncontrollably and crush either of them. Unfortunately, ideal wasn't the usual picture for him, so by necessity he'd gotten good at improvising.

Taking the handkerchief from his back pocket, he said, "This could get messy, and I don't want you breathing in any more of it than you have to."

"What about you?"

"I'll be fine. It might take a little doing, but I'm gonna lift this beam up. When you feel things loosen up under there, I want you to slide as far to your right as you can."

Clearly fighting his fear, the pastor nodded, determination in his dark eyes. Seth tied the handkerchief into place for him and asked, "Are you ready, sir?"

"Ready."

Seth yoked the beam on his shoulders and braced his legs for a test shove. The pile shifted but nothing big came crashing down, which told him the layers of debris were fairly well-balanced. Applying some more muscle, he managed to lever the beam up enough for the man to slide partway out from underneath.

"That's good," Seth told him as he carefully lowered the stack of splintered lumber. "Don't move anymore till we can get a backboard."

"I won't." He held absolutely still, which was a good sign. He was conscious and listening. Most people in this kind of situation wouldn't be doing much of anything.

"You're Ruthy's nephew Seth, aren't you?"

"Yes, sir."

"She goes on and on about you." Sighing, he closed his eyes. "I see now she's been holding out on us."

What exactly had she told her friends? Seth wondered. Shaking off the uneasy feeling the question caused him, he focused on getting the pastor out of the church before the building caved in on them.

Now that their position was slightly less precarious, Seth decided to make some more space for the EMTs to move around in. Bracing his hands on the beam that held up one side of the pile, he drove in with every bit of his strength and shoved the stack away with a deafening clatter.

The weight of it carried farther than he'd expected, tearing a hole through the side wall. Fortunately, the framing structure held, but it still wasn't quite what he'd had in mind.

He traded a look with the pastor. "Sorry about that."

"There's a leak behind that wall, anyway. We've been wanting to open it up and fix it for years." Through the dust hanging in the air, those dark eyes twinkled at him. "We could use your help with that."

As innocent as the offer seemed, Seth couldn't help feeling uncomfortable about being singled out this way. During his time in the desert, he'd been taught to blend in and disappear, so standing out in any way still felt like a bad thing to him. Harland was a completely different kind of place, he reminded himself. The people here were genuinely kind and helpful to each other. This was his life now—he just had to get used to it.

Something in the way Pastor Charles had phrased his request, making it so personal, made Seth want to agree even though he didn't know the details. In his experience, leaping before you looked could be deadly, so he hedged. "You need a contractor for a job this big. I'm just a carpenter."

"You know, son, I work for a carpenter who did some pretty impressive things."

The reference to the faith he'd abandoned made Seth's skin crawl. Before he could come up with a polite way to decline, two shocked EMTs appeared on the other side of the hole.

"We thought the whole place was coming down," one of them said with obvious relief. "You okay?"

"I am, but Pastor Charles needs some attention. You'll want a stretcher and a backboard, just to be safe."

The guy cocked his head. "You a doctor or something?"

Hardly in the mood for twenty questions, Seth gave him a stern glare. Fortunately, the EMT backed off, grabbing his partner before hurrying back to the ambulance. Waiting for them to come back would only annoy him, so Seth knelt down beside the injured man.

"How're you doing, sir?"

"A little sore, but I'll be good as new in no time," he replied with a grateful smile. "Thanks to you."

Seth wasn't used to being around to get credit for what he'd done, so the praise didn't settle well. "Just pitching in."

Fortunately, the medics showed up and saved him from having to make any more conversation. Because moving around in the wrecked church was dangerous, Seth helped steady things while they got their patient strapped in and off to safety. When the scene was as secure as it was going to get, Seth stepped through the hole he'd inadvertently created. Actually, it was a good thing he had. It was a much safer route out than the way he'd come in.

As the ambulance pulled away, out of the corner of his eye Seth noticed something that looked out of place. The red-and-blue emergency lights swirled through the vivid colors of a stained-glass window that had somehow survived the cave-in.

A scene of Jesus surrounded by animals, it suited the small-town setting perfectly. The winking effect made him think of the Christmas lights he and Lisa had strung at the diner the other day. He'd seen more than his fair share of carnage, and there had never been anything beautiful left behind.

Did it mean something, or was it just a lucky break? While he was considering the possibilities, Lisa appeared beside him.

"That was amazing," she breathed, admiration sparkling in her eyes. "I've never met a real live hero before."

"I was just in the right place at the right time," he said as they moved out of the path of two fire trucks.

"So was I, but I never could've gotten him out of there. He and his family will be incredibly grateful to you. Actually, the whole town will be. He means a lot to all of us."

Perfect, Seth grumbled silently. He'd come here to lend a hand at the diner, not be the center of a lot of unwanted, undeserved attention.

Sighing, he looked down at the pretty waitress who'd been so kind to him. "Could you do me a favor?"

"Sure," she agreed with a bright smile.

"Could you keep this quiet?"

"In Harland?" She laughed. "Are you serious? Everyone already knows."

"I really don't want that."

Clearly puzzled, she tilted her head like a curious cocker spaniel. "Why not?"

"I like being under the radar."

"What radar?"

He didn't know how to explain it to her, so he shook his head and started to walk away. When he heard her gasp, he whipped back around. "What's wrong?"

"Your shirt. Your shoulder."

Reaching over, he could feel that the

shoulder seam on his left sleeve had gotten torn during the rescue. That meant...

"I have to go." He backed away from her as if that would make her forget what she'd seen.

"Wait!" Pulling off one of her silver hoop earrings, she lifted the flap of his shirt and used the wire to fasten it to the remaining fabric. "That will cover it till we get to the hospital."

"No." The harshness in his tone made him wince. "I'm sorry, but I'm fine, really. Nothing to worry about."

"Seth, your hands are all cut, and you're bleeding in a dozen places. You at least need to clean up and get some bandages."

As more emergency vehicles raced toward the square, people started flooding in to see what was going on. Cornered and helpless, Seth's razor-sharp instincts were screaming for him to drop back and disappear. The problem was, there was no cover in this wide-open town square for him to slither into.

His skin crawled with cold sweat, adrenaline twisting his gut so hard he thought he'd be sick. Another quick survey of the area showed him he was completely out of options.

Swallowing the nausea, he turned to Lisa in desperation. "Will you help me?"

Chapter Three

Panic stiffened his expression, and his entire body looked ready to do battle. Lisa had never been in a war, but Seth reminded her of a trapped animal who was prepared to fight to the death rather than surrender.

But there was no enemy to engage, and he had nowhere to run, which left him no options at all. She sensed that he was on the verge of completely losing control, so priority one was to get him calmed down before that happened. She couldn't do that here.

The wild swings in his behavior—from heroic to panicked—were like nothing she'd ever seen, and she wasn't sure what to do. Then she recalled Ruthy taking his hand

and talking quietly, forcing him to listen. If she tried the same, would he go along or turn and run?

Lisa reached for his blood-streaked hand, half expecting him to pull away.

He didn't.

Instead, he clasped her hand firmly, as if he was holding on to a rope that could save him from falling into nothing. After the horrific view she'd gotten of his shoulder, his shadowy history only made her more curious about him. Maybe someday he'd trust her enough to tell her the truth about himself. For now, he needed her help. Despite her misgivings about him, Seth had taken an enormous risk to rescue a man he'd never met. She wasn't about to let him down.

"Come on," she said as calmly as she could manage. "Let's get out of here."

They started walking, and she slipped her cell phone from the pocket of her apron.

"Where are we going?" he asked.

"Hush." She punched a button and put a determined smile on her face. "Hey, Ruthy.

Just wanted to let you know everything's fine. Pastor Charles is a little banged up, and the EMTs are taking him to Kenwood Hospital just to be safe. Seth's walking me back to my place to check on Cleo. We should be back in about half an hour." After a pause, she laughed. "Yeah, you know how she is when the weather gets bad like this. I'll make up the time later. 'Bye."

She put the phone away, and he smiled down at her. "For a waitress, you're pretty good under pressure."

"It's not a lie," she informed him coolly. "I found my cat when she was about four weeks old, out in a bad thunderstorm. Ever since then she's been terrified of storms. I'll be glad if she comes out of hiding at all today."

Turning down a side street, she led him up a set of stairs and unlocked the door of an apartment wrapped on three sides by a wide porch. After being hammered by the wind for so long, the calm inside was a welcome change.

She loved her tidy studio, with its L-shaped

kitchen tucked in one corner and a small bathroom in the other. The garlands swagging from the ceiling were real, filling the open space with the outdoorsy scent of pine. Twined into them were long strings of ivy and tiny white lights that popped on when she hit the switch by the door. A nice contrast to the clouds outside, the effect was warm and inviting.

"Cleo?" Lisa called out, moving around in search mode. "The thunder's gone, baby. You can come out now."

It took her about two minutes to discover the cat was nowhere to be found. Hands on her hips, she declared, "I'll guess she'll turn up when she's ready."

Glancing around, Seth frowned. "Can she really get out of here?"

"There's a hole in the bathroom ceiling that goes up into the eaves. I've never checked, but I think she hides in there when she's scared."

Moving to the doorway, Seth peered into the bathroom. "Did it ever occur to you that if she can get out, other critters can get in?"

Lisa went into the kitchen and turned on the water to wash the dust off her hands. "Oh, it's not that big."

"I don't know. Mice don't need much of an opening."

"Cleo would take care of any that snuck in," Lisa assured him.

"How is she with bats?"

She'd just opened the cupboard where she kept the first-aid kit, and she stared over her shoulder at him. "Bats?"

"Not your favorite, huh?"

She shuddered as she pulled out the little box. "We have them out at the farm all the time. They're like rats with wings."

"If you've got some cardboard and tinfoil, I can make a plug for you to put in the hole after your cat comes back."

"I'm perfectly capable of doing that myself."

"Sorry," he apologized, holding up his hands in deference to her temper. "Didn't mean to offend you."

"Yeah, no one ever does." Sighing, she

said, "Have a seat. We need to get you cleaned up before anyone else sees you."

She motioned for him to sit at the kitchen table. Once she had a bowl of warm water, she joined him.

"This might hurt," she warned as she stirred some rubbing alcohol into the water.

"It's okay. I'm pretty tough."

She couldn't begin to imagine how tough he'd have to be to survive the injury she'd glimpsed before he turned away to hide it from her. While she was trying to think of something to talk about other than that, he gave her a warning look.

"Don't ask. I can't tell you."

"*Can't* meaning you can't stand to talk about it, or *can't* meaning you're not allowed to?"

Grimacing, he clamped his mouth shut and refused to answer her. But his eyes had gone that icy color again, and she decided she'd had enough of his emotional-freezer routine.

Making sure she had his full attention, very carefully she said, "That's your choice, but you should know I don't do dark and mysterious. Life is short, and I don't waste my time chasing after people who can't come out of themselves long enough to enjoy it."

He took a minute to absorb that, and his demeanor shifted slightly. "I'm not allowed to talk about it. Not with anyone."

What a horrible sacrifice to make, she thought wistfully. Unless that order changed, Seth would spend the rest of his life with part of himself locked in the past.

"That can't have been easy to admit," she said approvingly as she unwound a length of gauze to wrap around the large pad she'd set on his forearm. "Thank you for being honest with me."

"I wish—"

When his voice faltered, she glanced over at him. "What?"

"Nothing."

While she was dying to know what he wished, she realized this disillusioned man had coiled up tight for a reason. No amount of prodding would convince him to open up to her unless he wanted to. If that meant it would never happen, she had to accept that. She might not like it, but she really didn't have a choice.

He cleared his throat and said, "I wish I was more like you."

"Really?" Astonished by his revelation, she laughed. No one had ever told her that before. "Why is that?"

"Some folks can put their feelings right out there for everyone to see. You're one of 'em."

"Is that good or bad?"

"Good," he answered immediately. "Very good."

He gave her a shy smile that made her want to hug him. Maddening as he was, he had a vulnerability that made her want to put in a little more effort with him than she normally would. If he was anyone else, she'd shrug at his quirks and be nice but not pursue him as more than a casual acquaintance. But it was Christmas. Goodwill toward men and all that.

And there was something in the way

Ruthy had thanked her for being nice to him that made Lisa want to keep trying. Far from home, he needed a friend. She could do that.

"Something smells good." He complimented her on the spicy aroma wafting over from a Crock-Pot on the counter.

"Chili for supper tonight. It's great with Ruthy's corn bread. When the weather gets cold, I have it a lot because it's easy to make while I'm at work."

"I should try that sometime. Maybe you could give me the recipe."

"Two cans of stewed tomatoes, a packet of chili powder and a half-pound of browned hamburger." As she rinsed her cloth, she grinned over at him. "I'm not much of a cook."

"You've got me beat, that's for sure."

"You just need a little practice is all."

Yeah, Seth thought, *with a lot of things.* Like not getting tongue-tied when a pretty woman smiled at him the way Lisa was doing now.

"Y'know," she said while she rubbed salve into the worst cuts on his arms, "that whole roof could have caved in on you. God was really watching out for you."

He wasn't willing to reveal that he and God had parted ways long ago. "It wasn't as bad as it looked."

That wasn't entirely true, but he sensed that if he started debating religion with this very determined woman, it wouldn't end well. This was her house, and if he couldn't agree with her, the least he could do was not make her angry.

Uncertainty hung in the air between them, and he searched for a way to get past it. "So what does the rest of your week look like? Lots of Christmas shopping?"

Lame, lame, lame, a familiar voice in his head chided him. Fortunately, Lisa was more forgiving.

"Oh, I've been done for two weeks now," she replied as she rinsed out her cloth. "It's a good thing, because I'll probably be busy at the church."

Seth chuckled. "They didn't even have

Pastor Charles strapped on the gurney yet, and he was already trying to talk me into helping with the repairs."

"That sounds like him."

"I think he was a little loopy," Seth continued. "He asked me to head up the crew."

"Why is that loopy? You're doing a great job for Ruthy, and the way you rushed into that mess, you've got plenty of guts." She gave him an encouraging smile. "That's really all you need."

"I don't know. I've got a lot going on."

Pinning him with a no-nonsense stare, very quietly she said, "I've gone to Christmas Eve service in that church every year since I was born. I can't imagine it any other way."

The thought of her being so disappointed made him feel like a heel. It also made him feel as though he should explain his reluctance. "It's not that I don't want to help."

"Then what is it?"

The truth stuck in his throat, but he knew he owed her at least that much. After some hunting, he came up with an explanation he could live with. "I'm not very religious, so working on a church doesn't seem right."

As she wrapped a bandage around his left hand, she casually asked, "Is this non-religious thing a habit or something new?"

"I was raised in it, like you. It just doesn't work for me anymore."

"Any particular reason?"

"God quit listening to me."

Seth was horrified to hear that come out of his mouth. He'd never said it quite so bluntly, and it sounded bitter. Then again, he *was* bitter, so maybe that was reasonable. To his surprise, Lisa didn't chide him the way his mother often did. Actually, she didn't seem all that concerned.

Instead, she bathed him in a gentle, understanding smile. "I know it seems that way sometimes. God's timing isn't like ours, because He's been around so long and He can see so far into the future. He always hears us. He just doesn't always answer right away."

"Well, I got tired of waiting."

He'd endured three years of covert missions in the blazing sun, begging for divine help that never materialized, but Seth didn't want to get into that with her. Now he understood why smart people never discussed politics or religion with each other. It was the best way to remain friends.

"Maybe," she suggested as she tied off the bandage, "if you think of the project as a building instead of a church, you'll feel better about lending a hand."

When she connected with his eyes, the hopeful look on her face nearly did him in. Then logic kicked in, reminding him that he was treading on very thin ice.

He hated to disappoint her, so he said, "Maybe." While she started cleaning up his other hand, he ran his bandaged one over the mosaic tabletop. "This is really cool. I've never seen one like it."

"That's because I made it."

She made it sound as if it was no big deal, but Seth was impressed. Leaning forward, he studied the design. "Really? How?"

"I got the table for five dollars at a yard sale and crushed up some broken Spanish and Italian tiles Gus was throwing out. After that, I just had fun with it." Tying the last knot, she said, "All done. If that gash still looks nasty after you take the bandages off, I'll redo it for you."

"Thanks."

Standing, she walked the few steps to the kitchen and started putting her things away. While he waited, Seth wandered into the bathroom to check out the ceiling. After poking around for about thirty seconds, he found several waterlogged ceiling panels. A quick look around told him why.

"You don't have a fan in here," he called.

"Does that matter?" she asked from the doorway. "It's just me."

"Every bathroom needs an exhaust fan. You should have your landlord put one in."

Tilting her head, she gave him a get-real look, and he chuckled. "I'll bring my tools over tomorrow and take care of it." When her eyes narrowed, he amended his offer with, "If you want."

"I thought you had a lot going on." She tossed his flimsy excuse back at him with a healthy dose of sass to make sure he got her point.

He decided not to take the bait. "This is a basic drop ceiling. It'd take me about an hour to put in a fan and replace all the panels. You helped me out today. I'd like to return the favor."

"What about helping with the church? You don't have to be the foreman, just sign up for the crew. There's only three weeks till Christmas, and we need every set of hands we can get."

"I'll think about it." When she gave him a chiding look, he added, "That's the best I can do."

Lisa's expression told him she hated his nonanswer, and he glanced around her apartment, searching for a way to get back in her good graces. He found his inspiration on the walls. Every inch of them was filled with artwork, and he strolled around admiring each one in turn. When he spotted her signature at the bottom of one, he asked, "You painted these?"

Seth recognized it was a stupid question,

but it made her smile, which was a relief. After all, she was the only friend he had in this town. He didn't want her mad at him if he could avoid it.

"Yeah, they're mine. It's a hobby."

Paintings and sketches of various sizes hung everywhere, and in the corner he saw more paintings stacked on end like books. Bright landscapes were mixed with more subdued views of foggy and cloudy days. The people she'd painted had so much dimension and character, he felt as if he could walk up and talk to them.

On an easel stood a portrait in progress, with a picture tacked to the upper corner. The photo was faded, and he assumed it was fairly old. None of the six people in it looked familiar at first. Then the dark-haired woman caught his eye, and he did a quick comparison with Lisa.

"Is this your family?"

"Yes." She looked completely shocked. "You've only met me so far. What made you think that was us?"

"Her." He pointed to the woman holding

the adorable, laughing toddler instinct told him was Lisa. "She looks like you."

Some emotion he couldn't describe flooded Lisa's face, and for a few terrifying seconds, he thought she might cry. Instead, she amazed him with the most incredible smile he'd ever seen. How many did she have, anyway?

"That's my mother. She died of leukemia a few months after that picture was taken." Staring at the picture, she continued. "All us kids have a copy of it, but as you can see, they're not holding up well. I thought it'd be nice to do a full-size oil painting that would last forever. I want to have it ready to hang over the fireplace at our farm in time for Christmas."

Seth recalled her mentioning her father's death. He could only imagine how much the painting would mean to the Sawyers. "That's a real nice idea."

"I don't remember her at all." Lisa tapped her mother's face with a nail done in cotton-candy pink. "I'm having a terrible time getting her right."

"Check the mirror," he suggested. "She has darker hair and eyes than yours, but other than that, you look just like her."

Lisa beamed with pride. "That's the nicest thing anyone's ever said to me."

Normally, Seth would only vaguely understand what she meant. To his astonishment, her revelation did more than that. The part of him that he'd thought had died out in that nightmarish desert rustled, as if it were waking up from a long sleep.

Baffled by the sensation, he moved away from the easel and began flipping through the other canvases. "These are really nice. You should try selling them in a gallery or something."

"Oh, no." She shook her head with finality. "I'm a total amateur."

"I'm no expert but these look pretty professional to me. Did you go to art school or something?"

"Just practice," she said with a shrug.

Clearly, she was uncomfortable talking about her impressive talent, so he thought it best to let the subject drop. From the bathroom came a thud, followed by the most pitiful sound he'd ever heard. Somewhere between a howl and a moan, it bounced off the tiles in a mournful echo. Lisa hurried over with obvious concern, pausing in the doorway with a relieved smile.

"There you are." Going inside, her voice went all mushy as if she were talking to a child. "Were you scared, Cleo? I'm so sorry. Mama's here now, and the storm's over. You're gonna be just fine."

Still murmuring reassurance, she came back into the kitchen holding a miniature bobcat in her arms.

"Whoa. What is that?" he asked.

"This is Cleopatra, queen of the Nile." With a mischievous grin, Lisa angled the cat toward him. "She's a Maine coon."

Seth wasn't too fond of cats, and he eyed it suspiciously. "She looks like she could eat a coon."

"Not my Cleo," Lisa crooned, cradling the very fluffy ball of fur in her arms like a baby. Cooing some more, she rubbed noses and planted a kiss between its tufted ears. "She likes Ruthy's shrimp salad."

"Who doesn't?" he joked, chuckling as he shook his head. Deciding to risk his hand, he reached it out for the cat to sniff. She didn't bite it off, so he considered the experiment a success. When she rubbed her cheek against his fingers, he grinned. "I think she likes me."

"Incredible." Lisa stared up at him with a curious expression. "She hates everyone except for me."

Seth gave the cat a mock bow. "I'm honored, your highness."

Calmer now, Cleo dropped to the floor and sashayed over to the couch. Using it as a springboard, she jumped into the wide greenhouse window, settling on a carpeted perch among the potted herbs and flowers. She squirmed around a little, trying to find just the right position. Once she was satisfied, she surveyed the view below with what Seth could only describe as arrogance.

Perfect, he mused with another grin. The cat thought she owned the entire town. It didn't escape him that in the three days he'd been in Harland, he'd smiled more than he had in the past two years.

"That's quite a roommate you've got there," he said as he joined Lisa at the kitchen counter.

She pulled a ceramic bowl from the fridge. Covered in multicolored paw prints, Cleo's name was written across it in flowing script. Lisa set it on the floor, and Cleo came sauntering over for a snack.

"She's the best," Lisa commented as she ruffled the cat's long fur. "Warm and cuddly, and she's always happy to see me."

In the confession, he heard that Lisa had been lonely before she took in the stray kitten. There was something seriously wrong with this bright, engaging woman ever feeling that way. Since it wasn't his place to say anything like that, Seth followed his father's often-repeated advice for dealing with women. He kept his mouth shut.

Noticing a stack of travel folders on the counter, he motioned toward the colorful brochures. "Going somewhere?"

"Europe. I'm using some of the money my dad left me to book a nice, long tour in the spring," she explained with an excited-little-girl smile. "I can't wait."

"Have you decided where to go?"

"Not yet."

Leaning over, he fanned through the splashy catalogs and pulled out one called *Exploring the Emerald Isle.* "You'd like Ireland. It's wild and beautiful, and the people are real friendly."

"You've been there?"

"I've been to all those places."

Leaning on the counter, she looked up at him. "It sounds like you didn't enjoy them much."

Unwilling to dampen her enthusiasm, he didn't say anything. Unfortunately, she read him like a big, open book. The kind with lots of pictures.

Staring at him, she looked totally appalled. "I can't believe anyone blessed enough to visit all these fascinating countries would regret doing it."

Since he couldn't begin to explain it to

her, he settled on something vague. "Traveling gets old after a while."

"I've been to Charlotte, and I went to Chicago once to visit my big sister before she and her kids moved back here. I've always wanted to see some of the world, maybe even live in Europe for a while. Whenever I mention it to anybody, they just pat my head and say 'that's nice, honey.' I really hate that," she added, tilting up her nose in disdain.

"I can see why."

She rewarded him with an approving smile. "Thank you."

After that, they chatted some more about arts and crafts while Lisa tidied up. Seth kept waiting for her to ask about his wreck of a shoulder, but she didn't. While she rummaged around in the single closet and found him a dark blue T-shirt to wear, he expected her to mention what she'd seen.

Instead, she said, "That's the biggest shirt I've got, but I think it'll work. You can change in the bathroom, and then we should get you back to the diner. Ruthy will be worried sick when she hears you were the one who rescued Pastor Charles."

Seth's stomach plunged to the floor. "Nobody knows it was me."

"Trust me," Lisa told him with a grin. "Everybody knows it was you. That means Ruthy does, or she will soon. You need to show her you're okay."

It hadn't even occurred to him that his aunt would be worried about him. Feeling awkward and stupid, he stared down at the T-shirt in his hands.

"Seth?"

Out of pure, stubborn pride, he lifted his head and met those beautiful blue eyes.

"I don't know what's in your past," she continued, "and you don't have to tell me if you don't want to. But you're here now, and you're safe. Nobody in Harland means you any harm, least of all me. Now, go change your shirt and we'll walk back to the diner together. Okay?"

Her compassion drove that stupid feeling back a few steps, and he nodded. "Thanks."

He went into the bathroom and shut the

door. He'd just pulled the borrowed shirt on when he felt his phone buzzing in the pocket of his jeans.

Pulling it out, he read the caller ID before clicking it on. "Hey, Aunt Ruth."

"Where are you?" she demanded in an echoing whisper.

"Lisa's. You sound like you're in the storeroom," he teased.

"That's because I am."

"Why?"

"Don't come back here," she warned. "Folks are piling up in the diner, waiting to get a look at the town hero."

Suddenly, the situation wasn't so funny. The blind panic he'd felt earlier returned almost full force, and his pulse shot into hummingbird range. There was no reason for that, Seth chided himself.

You're here now, and you're safe.

Lisa's reassurance echoed in his mind, soothing his nerves.

"Lisa's on her way back there. I don't think I should hang out at her place without her."

"Come in the back gate," his aunt suggested. "Then stay up in your room. Once the hoopla settles, I'll take you home with me and make you a proper meal."

The thought of being trapped upstairs made Seth's skin crawl, but going to her house might actually be worse. Nice as it was, the chances of running into more Bentons were almost a hundred percent. After the emotional beating he'd taken today, Seth wasn't up to trading small talk with one of his happy, successful cousins.

So he chose the better of his two very unappealing options. "I'm kinda tired, so I think I'll just stay in my room."

"Sethy, are you okay?" she pressed. "The truth, now."

He bit back a groan. The childish nickname emphasized just how worried she was about him.

"I'm fine." Nudging the door open a crack, he peered out to find Lisa waiting by the front door. "Lisa's ready to go, so I'm on my way."

"All right," she relented. "And Seth?"

"Yeah?"

"What you did today was incredibly brave. I'm very proud of you."

With her praise ringing in his ears, he smiled and told her again he was on his way.

After making sure Seth got upstairs unseen, Lisa tied on a clean apron and pushed through one of the swinging kitchen doors into the diner. Way over capacity, the place was crammed wall to wall with busybodies who weren't even pretending they were there for any reason other than to gawk at Seth. Plastering a smile on her face, she grabbed an armload of menus and waded into the crush. If she played this right, she'd make enough in tips this week to cover her rent.

Or a few moonlit boat rides up the Thames, she thought with a grin.

"Lisa!"

She turned to find Priscilla Fairman waving to her from a corner table, where she sat with friends. Going on eighty-five, the petite, frail-looking woman had been the head of the Harland Ladies' League for the past forty years. Not to mention the town's gossip mill began and ended with her. If it was worth knowing, Priscilla knew about it. And made sure it was spread around at light speed.

"How are you today, ladies?" Lisa asked, handing each woman a menu. "Would you like to start off with some of our candy-cane tea?"

"Actually, dear," Priscilla replied, leaning in with an eager expression. "We're looking for information."

"Really?" Resting a hand on the back of a chair, Lisa faked complete brainlessness. "About what?"

"Seth Hansen, of course," one of the others said. "We heard you were the one who called 911, so you must know what happened."

Priscilla nodded. "When people ask, we want to make sure we have our facts straight."

Facts had absolutely nothing to do with it, Lisa knew. They just wanted to make sure they scooped their biddy friends who were trying to eavesdrop from another table.

She'd always had a soft spot for the Fairmans, so Lisa asked, "What would you like to know?"

"Did Seth really pull the roof off Pastor Charles?"

"A good chunk of it."

Dressed head to toe in classic Chanel, Helen Witteridge fanned herself with her hand. "Oh, my."

Lisa couldn't keep back a grin. Widowed four times, Helen prided herself on being a connoisseur of men. If Seth gave her the vapors, Lisa could only imagine the effect he'd have on the rest of the women in town. Of course, he'd have to come out of hiding first.

"Yeah," she agreed. "He's pretty strong."

She knew that for herself, having felt that strength when he shielded her from the storm. That sense of being completely safe crept into the front of her mind, and she did her best to ignore it. There was no sense in getting all gooey over Seth. There was a lot of baggage with that one, and Lisa liked her relationships simple. It made it easier to wiggle free when things had run their course and she wanted to move on. Besides, she was going to Europe in a few months. She had every intention of enjoying her foreign adventure to the fullest.

She took the ladies' orders while they peppered her with more questions. She answered them as truthfully as she could without making Seth sound like Superman. Because, having seen it with her own eyes, she couldn't blame anyone for making that mistake. What he'd done was astounding.

Finally, at about six o'clock everyone decided there would be no show, and the crowd dwindled to their regulars.

Ruthy came up beside Lisa and put an arm around her shoulders. "I called in reinforcements for supper. You've had a big day, and I know you're still worried about Cleo. Why don't you head on home?"

The weight of her tip pocket made Lisa hesitate. She hated to give up the money she'd make finishing out her shift. "I can stay."

"I want you to go, honey," Ruthy insisted with a warm smile. "I'll make up your tips between now and seven."

Lisa almost protested, then had to laugh. "How did you know?"

"You keep patting your pocket like you can't wait to go count all that money. Now, get outta here before I change my mind and make you clean the bathrooms."

Laughing, Lisa gave her boss a quick hug before heading out the door. The walk to her apartment was much quicker as the crow flies, so she turned the corner to cut across lots.

The dark sky had mellowed to a washed-out gray after the storm, and she paused to admire the determined sunset pushing through to lighten the gloom. It was almost as if the sky had worn itself out pummeling Harland and was looking forward to some peace and quiet, just like she was. Through the drifting clouds, she caught a faint glimpse of the full moon.

While she was looking up, she glanced at the apartment windows over Ruthy's Place. They were all dark, which struck her as odd. Seth was in one of them, alone, with the lights off? Maybe he didn't want anyone to know he was there, she reasoned as she resumed walking.

The question was, why? What haunted him so much that he'd basically run away from it to hide out in a town where no one but his aunt knew him?

The fact that his shoulder had been so badly mangled was a frighteningly obvious clue. Lisa thought of several scenarios that could have wounded him so badly, each worse than the one before it. As bad as that injury was, she'd gotten the distinct impression that it was only half of his problem.

Sadly, the other half was the kind he might never be able to solve.

Chapter Four

Early Thursday morning, Seth showered and dressed before checking outside his window. They didn't roll up the sidewalks at night, but they might as well have. With dawn still a half hour away, Main Street was completely deserted.

While he was there Monday, he'd noticed that Harland Hardware opened at 5:00 a.m. Right now it was quarter after. If he was quick, he'd get there and back without running into anyone.

He could hear Aunt Ruth in the kitchen preparing breakfast, singing along with some guy about Christmas being the most wonderful time of the year. Wanting to duck a bunch of questions he'd rather not answer, Seth went down the back stairs to avoid her. Unfortunately, the lock on the service entrance squealed, giving him away.

"Good morning, Seth."

Feeling like a kid caught sneaking out of his room, he turned to find her eyeing him with a curious look. "Morning."

"You can use the front door, you know."

"Didn't want anyone to see me."

She didn't ask why, since she knew. Instead, she asked, "Are you hungry?"

"I'll grab something when I get back. I want to get to the hardware store while things are quiet out there."

"I thought you had all your supplies for upstairs."

"I do. It's for Lisa."

As soon as the words jumped out of his mouth, he wished he could yank them back. His aunt's eyes crinkled with humor, and she tucked her hands in the pockets of her snowman apron as she leaned against the wall. "Really? And what does Miss Lisa need from the hardware store?"

Seth explained, trying to sound as though he was simply lending a lady a hand. He suspected Aunt Ruth would read all kinds of things into the extra job he'd taken on, and he didn't want her getting her hopes up. Nothing was going to happen between him and Lisa. With colder weather settling in, he was just trying to keep critters from invading her apartment looking for a warm place to spend the winter.

When he was finished, Aunt Ruth rewarded him with a proud smile. "That's very nice of you. Have Gus put it on my tab."

For some reason, Seth's back went up. People had been babying him for the past two years. While he recognized that their hearts were in the right place, it was time he put a stop to it. "I've got money."

She studied him for a few long seconds, then gave a single nod. That simple gesture of approval made him stand up a little straighter, proud of himself for the first time in recent memory.

"All right, then," she agreed. "Eggs or pancakes?"

That she didn't hassle him or go all gushy on him made Seth feel more like his old self, and he grinned back. "Both."

That afternoon, the diner was packed once again, and Lisa had her hands full with customers and gossip. Of course, all they could talk about was the damage around the area and Seth's stunning rescue of Pastor Charles. After school, she heard two boys waiting for milk shakes debating whether Seth was more like Spider-Man or Batman.

She imagined most folks had returned hoping for a glimpse of Ruthy's mysterious nephew, but the construction-type banging and sawing overhead told her he was safely tucked away upstairs. Normally, Lisa enjoyed the bustle of the diner, visiting with people to get caught up on the latest news. Today, though, it bothered her. Despite being the town hero, Seth obviously wanted to maintain his privacy. Why couldn't everyone respect that and give the poor guy a break?

Cranky as she was, she kept smiling and got through her shift as pleasantly as humanly possible. She was just tired, she told herself as she signed her time card and slipped out the back door. She'd make an early night of it and wake up tomorrow in a better frame of mind.

As she walked between buildings, she glanced up and saw Seth framed in an upstairs window. Hands braced on either side of the lacy curtains, he was staring out over the Christmas-card view of Main Street. Dressed in yet another faded T-shirt, he looked as though he wanted nothing more than to get out of that room.

Feeling sorry for him, Lisa waved to get his attention. His expression brightened immediately, and the grin on his face as he opened the window made her heart do a little flip. When he loosened up, the man had a truly amazing smile.

"Hey, there," he said as he leaned his elbows on the windowsill.

"Hey, yourself. I didn't see you today."

"I was working up here in the apartments."

"Yeah, I heard," she joked with a quick laugh. "I hope Ruthy brought you lunch."

"She did. It's pretty noisy downstairs, isn't it?"

"No big deal. You'll be done with all this work soon, right?"

"Soon," he agreed with a frown.

She couldn't imagine why that made him unhappy, but she forged ahead. "Y'know, the hermit routine is actually making people more curious about you, not less."

"I can't help that."

He added a pathetic sigh, and Lisa felt even sorrier for him than she had a minute ago. "What are you doing now?"

"Waiting till the diner closes so I can eat my supper in peace."

"Those apartments all have kitchenettes," she pointed out. "Don't you have any food up there?"

He shrugged as though it didn't matter much one way or the other. "I've been so busy, I haven't had time to buy any groceries. Aunt Ruth's cooking is way better than mine, anyway."

"I've got plenty of leftover chili," Lisa blurted without thinking. "You can eat with me if you want."

Cocking his head, he considered her offer. "You sure?"

"Totally. I've even got fresh bread and soda to go with it." She held up the takeout sack that held a loaf still warm from Ruthy's oven, hoping she sounded confident. Now that she'd made the impulsive offer, she knew retracting it would hurt his feelings. After the risk Seth had taken to help Pastor Charles, she'd never do that to him. "Whattya say?"

Seth deliberated a few more seconds, then gave her another knee-weakening grin. "I'll be right down."

He closed the window and locked it, and she heard his boots eagerly pounding down the back stairs.

"Good grief," she muttered, fanning herself with her hand the way Helen Witteridge had. Glancing toward heaven, she grinned. "You really outdid Yourself the day You made that one."

When Seth joined her, he was holding two large Harland Hardware bags and a beat-up metal toolbox that looked as though it had seen a lot of action.

"What's all that?" she asked as they started walking.

"I got a fan and some ceiling tiles for your bathroom."

To her knowledge, the man hadn't gone anywhere since the storm. If she hadn't happened along and invited him to supper, he'd still be hiding out in his room staring at the walls. It floored her that he'd gone to so much trouble to help her out.

"That was really sweet," she said, careful not to look right at him. Direct contact with her seemed to make him jumpy. "I'll pay you back."

"I'll trade you for the chili."

She sneaked a glance up at him, and he actually winked at her. His demeanor shifted faster than a summer storm, and she wasn't sure what to make of it. Normally, she took people as they came, without analyzing them too deeply. She didn't have that luxury with Seth. Right now he was being pleasant enough, but she'd glimpsed his darker side. She couldn't help wondering how long his sunny mood would last.

"There's really no hurry to fix the ceiling in there," Lisa told him as she unlocked her front door. "The patch I made is working fine."

"No time like the present," he replied, hoping he sounded cool.

The truth was, this spunky waitress had knocked him off balance when he first met her and he still hadn't fully recovered. Disturbing as his unexpected emotions were, he recognized that having any feelings at all, even unsettling ones, was better than the fog he'd been living in.

After studying him for a few seconds, she gave him a look that managed to come off as equal parts approval and dismay. "You're a stubborn one, aren't you?"

"I've been called worse."

It was the truth, but it wasn't like him to be so flip with people. Where had that one come from? he wondered. For some strange reason, Lisa had a knack for bringing out the best in him. He didn't know if that was good or bad, but since his stomach was rumbling for chili, he decided to reserve judgment for now.

Laughing, she reached into a cupboard for two bowls. "All right, you can fix my ceiling. But eat first. You've been working so hard, you must be starving."

"I was ready to fry up my boots."

He took the bowl she handed him and ladled chili into it. Offering it to her, he took the other one and filled it, too. While she sliced bread on a cutting board, he set their bowls on the pretty mosaic table and filled a couple of glasses with soda. He even remembered to fold some napkins and put them at each place. It was an afterthought, but he congratulated himself for thinking of it at all. It had been a long time since he'd paid much attention to things like napkins and dishes.

Cleo appeared from nowhere, blinking up at him as if she'd just woken up from a nap. Standing on her back legs, she wrapped her white snowshoe paws around his leg and rubbed her cheek on his jeans.

"Careful," Lisa warned with a laugh. "She's marking her territory."

"What?" Seth asked as he reached down to ruffle her fur. "She thinks I belong to her now?"

"Of course." The mischievous twinkle in Lisa's eyes contradicted her serious tone. "It's good to be the queen."

"And you're the princess. Guess I better watch my step around here."

They both laughed. Before long, Cleo got bored with him and sashayed into the living room and curled up on the sofa. Seth waited until Lisa sat down and then joined her. While they ate, she filled him in on her day. She said "crazy busy" several times, but she didn't seem to mind it all that much. The crowd she'd handled so deftly would have sent him into standing shock, and Seth was impressed with her breezy attitude.

When she stopped talking to sip her soda, he asked, "You really like your job, don't you?"

"Most of the time, but I know everyone I see every day. It's nice, but I'd love to meet some new people."

"You're a people person, then."

She nodded. "Totally."

Seth noticed she didn't ask him if he felt the same way. Then again, she was more than bright enough to figure that one out on her own. "You're from a big family. That must have something to do with it."

"I guess so. I'm the baby, so everyone was always telling me how to be, who to hang out with, stuff like that."

"Calling you 'princess.'"

She made a sour face. "That's my favorite. Anyway, when I moved out, I really liked being able to do what I want."

"Like art?"

"Yeah." Glancing over at the easel holding her latest project, she smiled. "I know my family doesn't get it, but it's important to me, so they pretend to understand." Focusing back on him, she added, "Like going to Europe. None of them would ever do that."

"Did you decide where to go yet?"

"Everywhere. My sister's keeping Cleo for me, so I can stay as long as I want." She nodded to a stack of foreign-language books on the counter. "I want to learn some Italian, French and Spanish. I figure I'm good for England, Scotland and Ireland, since they all speak English."

"Kind of." Seth recalled fighting his way through some of those thick Gaelic brogues and wondered how she'd fare with her Carolina accent. After a spoonful of chili, he said, "No matter where you go, you really only need to know how to say one thing in their language."

"Where's the bathroom?" she guessed with a cheeky grin.

He chuckled, then shook his head. "Do you speak English?"

"Oh, come on." She tilted her head in disapproval. "Where's the fun in that?"

"These days they have apps for your cell phone that record what you say and translate it into whatever language you need."

"I want to learn how to speak them myself," she insisted. "At least a little."

"You can't learn more than vocabulary and basic grammar from a book," he cautioned. "You have to hear an actual conversation so you know how it flows. You'd do better on one of those learn-a-language websites."

She rolled her eyes, reminding him of his twelve-year-old niece. "Ugh. Learn from a stranger? No, thanks." Suddenly, excitement lit her face, and she leaned toward him. "Do you speak any of those languages?"

"Sure, but—" When it dawned on him where she was headed, very firmly he said, "I'm not a tutor, Lisa. You need a real teacher, someone who knows how to break things down and explain them to you."

"I need someone who's actually been to

these places and talked to the people there."
For dramatic effect, she held up her hands
and looked all around. "Where am I going
to find someone like that in Harland?"

"There's a community college in Kenwood," he suggested desperately, keenly
aware that this sweet country girl had neatly
backed him into a corner. "You could take
some classes there."

Sitting back in her chair, she folded her
arms and gave him the look of a woman
who was accustomed to getting what she
wanted. "I want *you* to teach me. I'll pay
you if that's the problem."

That wasn't the problem at all. In fact,
Seth knew he'd enjoy spending time with
her, teaching her to speak those languages
well enough that they could discuss the
things that so clearly fascinated her. The
thought of it appealed to him way too much.
That was the problem.

His cool, well-honed logic finally kicked
in, giving him the ultimate out. "I can't.
When I'm done at Aunt Ruth's, I'm going
home."

Her enthusiasm vanished, and she looked down at her untouched bowl of chili. "Oh, that's right. Sorry, I forgot."

She switched to a less personal topic, but Seth could see she was disappointed. Based on his disastrous history, he'd made it a practice not to promise anything to anyone, no matter how small. The trouble was, his quick friendship with Lisa had tricked him into believing this time—and this place— could be different. But it wasn't.

Despite every attempt he'd made to break those old patterns, he'd still managed to let her down. He sat there trying to swallow his food while the hope he'd begun to feel evaporated. As his heart coiled around the cold, hard truth, he knew he had no choice but to accept it.

Hard as he'd tried to correct the bleak course his life had taken, nothing had changed.

Chapter Five

༺

Friday morning, several construction trucks and a good-sized flatbed holding a bulldozer rumbled down Main Street. Lisa stopped clearing one of the window tables and watched to see where they were going. When they turned into the lot beside the damaged church, she headed outside for a closer look. *Picking up the pieces,* she thought with a smile. That was Harland for you.

When someone shouted her name, she turned to see her brother John dangling out the passenger window of a dark blue pickup. Their big brother, Matt, yanked him back into the cab, but she could hear

John laughing as they swung into the lot and parked beside several other farmers' pickups.

"Funny time of year for a parade," Seth said from the doorway behind her.

It was one of the few bits of humor she'd heard from him, and she was impressed. Maybe hanging out with her was loosening him up a little. "We're rebuilding our church. Even Mother Nature can't keep us down for long. A heavy-construction company came in yesterday to brace everything, and last night the inspector cleared us to start repairs."

He gave her a sidelong look. "How do you know all this?"

"Ruthy's Place is the hub of Harland," she replied with a smile. "We know everything that goes on in this town, sometimes even before it actually happens."

Chuckling, he shook his head and looked back out to the street. "Good to know."

The procession of trucks continued for almost a mile, and as the two of them watched each one pull in to park near the church,

Seth whistled in appreciation. "With all that help, we oughta be done next week."

Convinced she'd heard wrong, she stared up at him, which he didn't notice because he refused to look at her.

"We?" she echoed.

It took him a few seconds, but when he finally looked down at her, he shrugged. "Pastor Charles called yesterday and said he really needed my help. The other contractors he would've asked are busy and can't be on-site all the time. With me right across the street, it just makes sense for me to do it."

"Oh, Seth, that's awesome!"

Delighted by his change of heart, she gave him an impulsive hug. He stunned her by returning the gesture. Having those strong arms wrapped around her felt wonderful, and she cuddled in for one blissful moment before he stiffened and pulled away.

His eyes had shifted to that icy color she'd learned to be wary of. Because she still wasn't sure what that was all about, she decided it was best to forget their unexpected embrace. "We're doing lunch for the volunteers, so I'm headed over to see what folks would like. Do you want to come with me and meet your crew?"

"Sure." He hesitated, then fell into step beside her. "How's Pastor Charles doing?"

"When we get there, you can ask him yourself."

"Should he be up and around already?" Seth asked with a scowl.

"Probably not, but when he heard about everyone coming in today, he told Ruthy he'd be there, too, at least for a little while."

When they arrived at the site, someone was backing a front loader off its flatbed. Lisa recognized a couple of local contractors talking to men and women dressed in hard hats, pointing here and there to get them organized. A crane was lifting pallets of lumber from a long truck to stack them neatly beside an enormous Dumpster that was half-full of debris.

Seth assessed their progress with an approving look. "They've gotten a lot done already. Looks like they know what they're doing."

"Most of them, anyway," she laughed as her brothers headed their way. "These two, I'm not so sure."

"What?" John asked with an innocent expression. "I can swing a hammer with the best of 'em." Sticking out his hand, he added, "John Sawyer. This is my big brother Matt."

Lisa kept an eye on Seth while they shook hands all around. She knew it was crazy to feel protective of such a big, strong guy, but she felt it all the same. Wounded in more ways than one, he struck her as someone who needed every friend he could get. While he traded small talk with her brothers, she noticed that his genetic shyness seemed to be fading. She didn't know him all that well, but she was proud of him.

"What'd ya bring her for?" John asked him, nodding at Lisa. "The only thing she's good for is distracting the guys when they're supposed to be working."

"For your information," she informed

him haughtily, "I'm here to take a poll and find out what the crew wants for lunch. Ruthy's donating the food, and she wants to make sure people get their favorites."

"Long as you don't cook any of it," he teased, "we'll be fine."

Blowing out an exasperated sigh, she rolled her eyes. "There's absolutely nothing wrong with my cooking."

"Best chili I ever had," Seth put in.

Looking for all the world like a displeased grizzly bear, Matt folded his arms and pinned Seth with an unmistakable stare. He didn't say anything, but his overprotective meaning came through loud and clear. To his credit, the soft-spoken handyman didn't back down from Matt the way most folks did. He just stood there and took it.

"Back off, big brother," Lisa scolded him. "I had a friend over for supper. Deal with it."

Fortunately for all of them, Pastor Charles picked that moment to come over and say hello.

"Seth, so good to see you!" With both

hands, he shook one of Seth's, a delighted smile lighting his face. "I wanted to thank you again for your help the other day."

"How are you feeling?" Seth asked easily, making it plain that Matt didn't bother him in the least.

"Just fine. The doctor says I'll be right as rain in time for our Sunday service. It'll be at Ruthy's," he added, glancing at the other three. "Priscilla Fairman is spreading the word, and I hope you and the rest of the family can all be there."

"Absolutely," Lisa promised, her brothers nodding their agreement.

"Marvelous. I can always count on the Sawyers." Resting a hand on Seth's arm, he said, "If you'll follow me, I'll introduce you to your crew."

"You're in charge?" John asked with a grin. "Seriously?"

Seth answered with a grin of his own. "You ever try to tell this man 'no'?"

"Yeah, I see what you mean."

As the two of them strolled ahead with the pastor, Matt and Lisa followed.

"Seth seems like a good guy," Matt commented in his usual offhand way.

"The way you were glaring daggers at him, no one would ever guess you liked him."

"Just testing, baby doll. You know that."

"I really wish you'd quit calling me that," she huffed. "I'm grown-up now."

Laughing as if that was a wonderful joke, he hugged her around the shoulders. "I'll try. So what do you know about our foreman?"

"Not much." She relayed what Ruthy had told her, adding, "I get the feeling he's searching for something, but I'm not sure what."

"You'll figure it out," Matt assured her as they joined the assembling volunteers. "You always do."

Maybe rebuilding the church would help, she mused. It was a huge responsibility, but Pastor Charles seemed totally comfortable with Seth leading the project. Seth had certainly shown enough nerve to lead a construction crew made up of farmers, contractors and construction workers who basically knew what they were doing.

At least, she hoped so. He was so insecure around people, she hated to consider what a blow it would be to his confidence if he failed at this.

His heart in his throat, Seth waited while Pastor Charles climbed a set of temporary stairs and turned to face the crowd. There had to be over a hundred people there, but when he held up his arms for quiet, you could have heard a pin drop in that parking lot.

Man, this guy was good.

"First, I want to thank the group who came in here yesterday to tarp our open roof and make things safe for us to start our repairs." After winging a broad smile around, he continued. "Second, as unlikely as it might seem, we *will* celebrate Christmas Eve in this church. We may be wearing coats and gloves, but there will be a roof over our heads. More than that, I can't promise, but I'll be here. I hope you'll all be here with me."

A cheer went up, punctuated by whistles and rebel yells that seemed strangely perfect for this ragged crew. Some of them were obviously pros, but most were parishioners offering their time and energy to help rebuild their church. Even to a battered heart like Seth's, it was a touching sight.

When they settled down, the preacher went on. "For those of you who live in caves, I'd like to introduce the remarkable young man who came to my rescue when I needed him most. He has a great deal of experience rehabbing old buildings, and he's graciously agreed to head up this project for me. Seth Hansen."

The shouts of approval that welled up from the crowd were unnerving for someone so accustomed to doing his job and slipping away unnoticed. As he acknowledged their welcoming gesture, Seth admired how the pastor had cleverly sidestepped any protests about his choice of foreman. By making it a personal favor to himself, he'd ensured that no one would resent a stranger being in charge.

The man really knows how to talk to people, Seth thought. It was a handy skill for the leader of a church. Or a foreman. Diplomacy wasn't his strong point, but he'd committed to the job and he'd do everything he could to make things run smoothly.

Fortunately, the pastor didn't force Seth to go up on the platform and address the crowd. Instead, he reached behind him and took something from someone near the steps.

"Just one more thing, and then I'm done." Turning to Seth, he handed him a bright blue hard hat with "Hansen" stenciled on the front and back in bold black letters. "Welcome to the crew."

The crowd lifted their own hard hats, fishing caps and ball caps in response, and everyone cheered again. Up front, he noticed the Sawyers and smiled when John gave him a thumbs-up. Sandwiched between her towering brothers, Lisa beamed at Seth as if he'd just won the NASCAR championship.

Her encouragement melted a little more of the ice that had formed inside him over the past few years. She'd done so much for him in the short time he'd known her, and it felt good to repay some of her kindness by helping to repair the church she loved. If heading up this hodgepodge construction crew made her happy, Seth figured any trouble it caused him would be well worth it.

"Oh, come on, Seth." Leaning over the lunch counter, Lisa gave him a brilliant smile. "My family always gets together for Friday-night supper. Southern barbecue, corn bread and lots of Sawyers for company. After the long day you had, you can't do better than that."

"I do fine on my own." Hoping to avoid her gaze, he looked down to arrange his tools in their box and close the lid. She didn't say anything, but he could feel her watching him. Despite his best efforts, he couldn't resist glancing up.

Folding her arms, she nailed him with a knowing look. "You have plans?"

"No."

Her baffled expression told him she couldn't understand why it was so hard for him to mingle with other people. Her offer to include him in their family supper was sweet, just like she was. He was beat, but he hated to admit to her that the day of organizing the job site and getting to know his crew had stretched him far past his endurance for socializing.

"My family won't ask you about what happened the other day," she promised. "We'd just like to have you out for a meal."

"My truck's in the shop." The look she gave him clearly said she considered that the lamest excuse she'd ever heard. "Really, it is. You can call and find out for yourself."

"I'm done here at five. Just meet me out front and I'll drive us to the farm."

Since the day he met her, she'd been nudging, pushing, pulling and downright bullying him into doing things he'd never planned on. Nicely, of course, but the cute smile didn't mask the determination in her eyes. Why she'd made a project of him, he couldn't say. The fact that she believed he was worth all this effort made him feel something he hadn't been in a long, long time.

Happy.

"You're sure it's okay?" he asked.

"Absolutely."

She sounded confident enough, so Seth finally relented. "Okay. Thanks for the invitation," he added when he realized he'd almost forgotten.

"You're welcome." Giving him another amazing smile, she headed into the kitchen.

Suddenly, he remembered he didn't have anything to wear that didn't look as though it had been painted, torn or run over by a bulldozer. Since he was more or less done for the day, he poked his head into the storeroom.

"Need anything else today, Aunt Ruth?"

"Not a thing," she said, waving him out. "Go on and get outta here."

Her response made him suspicious, and he narrowed his eyes. "Eavesdropping again?"

"My nephew, my restaurant. I prefer to call it a vested interest."

Shaking his head, he pulled back from the doorway. When she called his name, he glanced over his shoulder.

"Do you have a jacket?" she asked. "It's supposed to get chilly tonight."

"Yeah, I heard something about that. I'm not six, y'know."

His aunt laughed. "I'll try to remember that. Have fun, Sethy."

He cocked his head at her, and she laughed again. "Sorry."

"You're just like Mom," he told her. "Always worrying."

That comment blew the smile right off her face, and she put down her clipboard before coming forward to meet him in the doorway. "We adore you, honey, and we know you're still hurting. It makes us overprotective sometimes, but we do it out of love."

"I know." Smiling to ease her frown, he kissed the top of her head. "But I think I'm finally doing better."

Her blue eyes twinkled with a knowing look. "Our Lisa does have that effect on people."

Seth groaned. "I'm not ready for anything like what you're thinking."

She gave him a long, steady look. "Katrina was a long time ago, and she wasn't strong enough to deal with your past. Lisa is."

"There are days even I can't face up to it, and I'd never ask a woman to take that on. It wouldn't be fair."

Before she could continue their pointless argument, he pulled back and headed for the door.

After opening the driver's door of Lisa's tiny yellow hatchback for her, Seth carefully folded himself into the passenger seat.

"Sorry," she apologized as she started the engine. "It's a little snug."

"No problem." He slid the seat back to the max and reclined it to give his legs some more space. Once she searched around and settled on a radio station, they drove up Main Street and out to the highway.

Seth hadn't been in Harland long enough to do any exploring, so he hadn't been outside the town limits yet. A couple of miles beyond the immaculate old houses and yards decorated for Christmas, there was a lot of nothing. Well, not nothing exactly, he corrected himself.

Fields plowed under for the winter rolled out like dark brown carpets, and he noticed several deer nibbling at a few remaining cornstalks. A fox spotted Lisa's car, and Seth thought it was actually racing along the road to see if it could beat them to wherever they were going. After about half a mile, it veered off and loped into a nearby stand of trees.

The air had a nip to it, but after breathing in joint compound and construction dust all day, it felt crisp and fresh to him. The muted colors of trees all around added to the picture, and he couldn't remember when he'd seen anything more perfect.

Lisa pulled into a dirt lane marked with a sign that read Sawyer Farm. The driveway wound between two lines of weathered wood fences shaded by massive oak trees that must have been around since before the Civil War. At the other end stood a sprawling white house bordered by generous porches twined with climbing roses and ivy. On the back landing was a black Lab who lifted its head from its paws as they approached.

"That's Tucker," she explained. "He's our welcoming committee."

Apparently, he recognized Lisa's car. The dog went bonkers, barking his head off while he galloped out to meet them. He ran a couple of laps around the parked car, then spun in circles before settling on his haunches. Even though he was in one place, his tail thumped the ground with barely contained excitement.

"He's real glad to see you," Seth commented.

"Tucker wears his heart on his collar. That's what I love most about him."

"Does Cleo know you're a dog person?" he teased.

"No, and don't you dare tell her. She'd be crushed."

Lisa opened her door, and the Lab ducked under it to greet her. Cooing and gushing, she ruffled the fur under the star-spangled bandanna he wore around his neck, then flopped his ears back and forth playfully. Seth could only describe the dog's expression as a big boy-am-I-glad-you-came smile.

"I forgot to ask," Lisa said hesitantly. "Are you good with dogs?"

Seth cringed at what should have been a completely unnecessary question. Then again, considering his odd behavior at times, he couldn't blame her for asking. So he deflected the awkwardness he suddenly felt with a grin. "Long as they're good with me."

"Tucker's our character barometer," she

told him as they got out of the car. "If he likes somebody, we know they're okay."

"Labs are pretty friendly as a rule. Who doesn't he like?" Seth asked as he hunkered down to let the dog get a good whiff of him. Apparently satisfied, Tucker flopped onto his back in a shameless demand for a belly rub.

"Marianne's ex. The nasty FedEx guy. The punk who used to throw rocks at the neighbor kids while they waited for the school bus. I'm not exactly sure what happened, but his mom drives him to school now."

Looking at the tongue hanging out of Tucker's mouth, it was hard to believe he could put a bully on the run. Of course, you couldn't always judge a hound's demeanor by its slobber. Seth's sister and brother-in-law had four Labs, and they were intelligent, protective creatures, especially around the kids. He wouldn't mess with one of them if he had a choice.

Standing, he admired the rolling acres that surrounded the farmhouse. They seemed to go on forever, and he could only imagine what it took to maintain it all. "This place is amazing. I didn't think family farms like this existed anymore."

"It's not easy." She pointed into the distance where two tractors with headlights on were plowing under cornstalks. "My brothers and brother-in-law work like crazy, and it's still barely enough to keep us in the black. We all pitch in where we can."

"After putting in six hours at the church, they came home for more?"

"Trust me, all those people did the same. There's no slackers in this town."

"That's what it takes," Seth agreed, following her toward the back door. "A good team can accomplish a lot if they set their minds to it."

"I don't know if you're looking for more work, but we can always use help here in the spring."

"And the summer, fall and winter?"

She laughed, and he drank in the sound. Bright and fresh, it made him think of daisies. The uncharacteristically poetic impression rattled him, and he tried to shake it off. "Thanks for the offer. I'll think about it."

"You already passed Matt's intimidation test. After that, it's cake."

The smell of the promised barbecue wafted through the screen, getting thicker as Seth pulled the door open. As they stepped into the Sawyers' kitchen, he admired the workmanship on the cabinets that were obviously original to the house. Done in shades of cream and sage, the large room was ringed with windows and dominated by a rough-hewn table that had been worn smooth over the years. With a bench on one side and chairs around the others, it was set for a family supper.

Even though he wasn't a Sawyer, they'd made a place for him at their table, and Seth felt pleased to be included. As he was admiring the intricate carving on the crown molding, their furry escort zoomed past him and made a beeline for the huge pot bubbling on the stove.

"Tucker, down!"

As if he were a little kid caught with a handful of forbidden candy, the dog dropped to the floor, getting as low as physically possible. Through the archway walked a slender woman dressed in khakis and a flowery blouse.

When she saw Seth, she smiled and came forward with her hand out. "You must be Seth."

"Yes, ma'am."

"Really, don't do that," she chided with a laugh. "I'm Marianne Collins, and if you call me Mrs. anything, I'll sic Tucker on you."

"Yes, ma'am. Marianne," he amended quickly. "Thanks so much for having me."

Some very inventive shouting was coming from the barn closest to the house, and she sighed. "Just ignore that. My husband, Ridge, is working on a tractor that should've gone to the Smithsonian years ago."

"I'm pretty good with stuff like that. Maybe I can give him a hand."

"Please."

She motioned him toward the door, and Seth gladly took the out. Lisa was great, and her sister seemed nice enough, but his small-talk skills left a lot to be desired. Helping a guy fix something, though. *That* he could handle.

"Like someone knitted his shoulder back together," Lisa finished with a shudder. "How could anyone survive an injury like that?"

Marianne set two cups of tea on the table next to a plate of her famous raspberry bars. "People can do a lot of things when they have to."

"That reminds me," Lisa said. "How are you feeling these days?"

"Sick as a dog." Looking a little green, Marianne pushed her tea away. "Nothing helps."

"That's what you get for letting Ridge talk you into that vacation in the Caymans."

"It sure was fun, though." Marianne added the kind of smile they hadn't seen much until she met the fun-loving pilot who'd managed to steal her well-guarded heart. "Just the two of us on the beach, watching those incredible sunsets."

"It's good to enjoy that kind of stuff while you can."

"Tell me about it." Marianne's complexion paled, and her voice took on an uncharacteristic whine. "It's not fair. Caty's sailing along like it's nothing. She'll probably have another four months of maternal glow, the world's quickest labor and be back in her law office the next day, carrying their baby in a sling."

"You never know, I guess. That's why I have Cleo. She cleans herself and I don't have to send her to college."

Despite the complaints, Marianne smiled, resting her hand on her still-flat stomach. "I know, but I wouldn't give up Kyle and Emily for all the cats on earth. They can't wait to meet our new little Collins. If the four of us can just agree on a name, we'll be all set."

"What are the ideas?"

"Kyle likes Payton, as in Walter Payton the football player."

"Of course he does," Lisa commented, rolling her eyes. The male species was so predictable. Sports and cars. Even if you could coax them to the theater, they fell asleep before the first act was over. "What about Emily?"

"She likes Jasmine and Belle."

"Disney princesses, that figures. What about Ridge?"

"He likes the solid, old-fashioned names. Michael, Andrew. Ethan," she added with a little smile.

"For Dad." When Marianne nodded, Lisa said, "They never met, but he knows it would mean a lot to you. That's one great guy you found, Mare."

"There's still a few of them out there, you know," she advised in her big-sister tone. "You just have to keep an open mind."

"My mind is completely open. It's the selection that's closing up."

Marianne clucked at her. "That's our little Lisa. Waiting for her knight in shining armor to ride up and carry her off to his castle."

Lisa sent her a mock glare. "I'm not little, and I'm not waiting for anyone. I'm just not ready to give up everything for some guy."

"That's not how it works. Sure, you lose some of your independence, but you get a lot in return."

"Like what?"

"Someone who loves you, no matter what," Marianne explained with a gooey smile. "I never expected to fall in love again, but Ridge changed all that for me. If you give someone a chance, it will happen for you, too."

"You've got a great life," Lisa agreed, "but you're stuck here in Harland. That's not for me."

"Trust me." Standing, Marianne took Lisa's cup to refill it from the teakettle on the stove. "Someday it will be."

"Well, it won't be with anybody from around here. These guys just aren't what I'm looking for."

"Which is what?"

Lisa took a few moments to frame her answer so she wouldn't sound like some flighty teenager. "Strong, but sweet. Smart, funny. Adores me shamelessly. You know, the usual stuff."

"You've dated a dozen guys like that," Marianne pointed out, rejoining her at the table. "But none of them stuck. There must be something else."

Lisa shrugged, and her gaze drifted through the archway that led into the warm, inviting living room. Somewhere in the distant future, she wanted to have family pictures scattered around the way Marianne did. Her eyes settled on the oversize portrait Marianne's wedding photographer had given them as a gift. Dressed to the nines, Ridge and Marianne stood behind Kyle and Emily, smiling at the camera the way they had that entire day. They all looked so happy, like the beautifully matched set God had meant for them to be.

She'd have that, too, Lisa promised herself. As soon as she found the white knight she'd been searching for since she was old enough to appreciate the concept of falling in love.

The problem was, she'd have to go somewhere else to find him. Guys like that just didn't exist in Harland, North Carolina.

"That's it," Ridge gritted through his teeth, straining to keep tension on the new drive belt. "Hold it right there."

Seth did as he was asked, keeping the assembly steady while Ridge coaxed the rubber belt around several pulleys that were stamped with the year they were made. 1925. Seth couldn't believe the tractor was still intact, much less a piece of equipment the Sawyers relied on to help them run their farm.

When he was finished, Ridge pulled himself up to the rusty seat and crossed his oil-stained fingers. "Here goes nothin'."

When he set the throttle and turned the key, the engine groaned and belched out a huge puff of black smoke. Sighing, he fiddled with the choke and tried again. This time, the old motor caught and let out gradually lighter smoke. Ridge made some adjustments, and it settled into a throaty rumble.

"Touchdown!" Ridge yelled, hopping down like a kid who'd just gotten a go-kart for Christmas. "That's what I'm talking about."

"How they've kept this thing running all this time is beyond me," Seth commented when they stepped back.

"I think the Sawyer boys all inherit some kind of mechanical gene." The man wiped his hand and held it out. "Thanks for your help. I really needed an extra set of hands, and my son's got math homework to do."

"Not a problem."

"We'll let her run awhile, make sure she's not gonna blow up or something."

"Okay." On the far side of the barn, Seth noticed a partially built biplane. "Is that yours?"

"Her name's *Ann Marie,*" Ridge said proudly. "Marianne wouldn't let me name a wreck after her, so I flipped it around. She's a World War II Boeing Stearman. Another year, we'll be flying."

"Really?" Seth surveyed the pile of parts doubtfully. "I'll take your word for it."

Ridge laughed. "Come on over and check her out."

Lisa's brother-in-law was obviously proud of his plane, explaining how he'd refurbished one with his grandfather and used it for crop-dusting and aerial tours. Then he traded it to a collector who had connections that could get Marianne's scheming ex-husband out of her life forever.

"That's amazing," Seth commented. "You gave up a lot for her."

Ridge waved it off as if it was nothing. "Grandpa found this one and gave it to me as a wedding gift so Kyle and I could restore it together. I figured it was God's way of telling me I did the right thing."

Religion again. Seth chafed at the mention of faith, but he kept his objections to himself. Fortunately, he was saved from more conversation by the roar of tractors approaching the barn's side door. They were moving pretty fast, and as they bounced over the rough ground, he could hear the drivers laughing.

They stopped just outside the door, and two very dusty Sawyers jumped down.

"No fair!" John hollered, pointing for emphasis. "You cut me off at the south end."

"You said no rules, Goldilocks."

Framed by the glare of the headlights, John folded his arms and gave his big brother a mock warning look. At least, Seth hoped it was a mock one.

"You cheated, Matt," Ridge chimed in. "Just admit it."

"Nobody asked you, flyboy." Matt cocked his head, and a grin brightened his grimy face. "You got that dinosaur running? Nice work."

The flip from intimidation to praise was quite a sight, and Seth braced himself when those dark blue eyes landed on him. "Nice to see you again, Seth."

"Same here." He hoped keeping it short would make him sound more confident. Because, honestly, this guy scared him. Seth had sisters of his own, and he understood the protective-brother routine. The thing was, these two farm boys could probably take him apart if they wanted to. If they quit arguing long enough, that was.

"Couldn't have replaced that belt without him," Ridge said. "Came out and jumped right in to help me."

"That was cool of you." John's face broke into a blinding country-boy grin. "I'm going back to my place to get cleaned up. See you at supper."

He and Matt left the barn together, still debating who'd won their race.

Ridge chuckled. "What a pair."

"I met them in town earlier, and John seemed real friendly. Matt, I'm not so sure about."

"Yeah, him you need to watch out for. We're best friends, and he made it clear if I did anything out of line with Marianne, my life wouldn't be worth living. He's old-school, right down to his boots. You hurt his baby sister, he'll take you somewhere only the buzzards will find you."

Seth angled a look at the pilot, figuring

he was just kidding. Judging by Ridge's somber expression, he was deadly serious.

"Thanks," Seth replied. "I'll keep that in mind."

Chapter Six

"So, they didn't eat you alive or anything," Lisa teased when Seth came into the kitchen.

She'd kept busy chatting and helping Marianne with supper, but the whole time she'd been a little worried about Seth stranded out in the barn with all that testosterone. She hadn't brought many men to the farm for supper, and she hated to consider the grilling he must have gotten tonight.

"Not quite." Hanging his denim jacket on a free peg by the door, he gave her a wry grin. "They debated roasting or broiling me at one point, though."

Completely stunned, she stopped filling

corn muffin cups in midpour. "Did you just make a joke?"

His grin faded. "Is that a problem?"

"Not a bit." She regretted making him feel self-conscious. "Those two have been scaring guys off for years is all. They're pros."

"Remember Henry Gruden?" Marianne asked while she pulled drinks from the fridge. "They lived two miles away, and John chased him all the way home after he got fresh with you."

Lisa wrinkled her nose in disdain. "He deserved worse."

"What happened?"

While the question sounded innocent enough, Seth's normally calm voice bristled with a note of warning. He was so protective, he made Tucker seem laid-back. Lisa couldn't decide if she liked it or not, but she knew she'd never want that intense, icy stare aimed at her.

"Nothing," she replied with a shrug. "It's ancient history."

"How ancient?"

"Twelve years. You know how teenage boys are."

Seth gave her a long look, then apparently chose to let it go. Deciding it was best to move on, Lisa shoved a full muffin tin at him. "Put this in the oven, please."

For the first time since she'd met him, he did something without hesitating. It was only sliding a pan into the oven, but still. He'd made some serious progress in the past few days, and despite her irritation, she was impressed.

Dusting cornmeal into the sink, she turned on the water to wash her hands. "So I heard a lot of banging upstairs this afternoon. How's it going?"

"Fine. I replaced the floor in one of the back apartments today, and tomorrow I'll do the other one."

"On a Saturday?" she asked, frowning. "Why?"

Leaning back against the island, he folded his arms. "Repairing the church is a huge job, and that's going to take a lot of time. Aunt Ruth's got new tenants coming in after New Year's, so those rooms have to be ready, too. Besides, the sooner I finish, the sooner I can move on."

"To what?" Lisa asked without thinking. It wasn't any of her business what was next on his agenda, and she felt her face heating with a very uncharacteristic blush. "I mean, if you don't mind me asking."

He shrugged. "Whatever. It's not like I have a schedule or anything."

Why didn't he? she wondered. A grown man, he didn't seem attached to anything—or anyone—except his parents and Ruthy. It just didn't seem right to her.

"You could go home for a while," she suggested, facing him while she dried her hands. "I'm sure your family misses you."

"Not really. I call them every day."

That was news to her. She'd spent a good amount of time with him and had never heard him make a phone call. "So, where is home?"

He hesitated, as if answering the question made him uncomfortable. "Fayetteville."

This was the closest she'd gotten to coaxing any even remotely personal information from the enigmatic handyman. "That's near Fort Bragg, isn't it?"

Grimacing, he gave a single nod that looked as though it required incredible effort. As it had the first time she saw him, his jaw tightened as if he was fighting against something. Lisa prayed it wasn't her. He had enough problems without her causing more.

"It's a nice area," she commented lightly, hoping to break the sudden tension between them.

"Yeah, it is."

Apparently, that was all she'd be getting out of him for now. Trying not to take his skittish behavior personally, she took a large bowl from the cupboard and handed it to him. "How are you with a salad?"

Most of the sternness left his features, and he gave her a little grin. "Making or eating?"

She laughed, and the emotion that flashed in his eyes made her heart leap into her throat. He looked desperate, almost, as if he was clinging to her to keep from drowning in this sea of strangers he'd found himself in. It was unsettling, to say the least.

When the buzzer on the dryer went off, Marianne set the sweet tea on the table and artfully skirted the two of them. "I've got whites to fold. Can you keep basting for me, Lisa?"

Still watching Seth, Lisa nodded. "Sure."

After the porch door closed behind her, Lisa asked, "Seth, is something wrong?"

His expression grew wary, and he half turned his head away from her. "Why?"

"You were just staring at me. Did I say something to upset you?"

"No." After a quick sigh, he rubbed his neck and met her eyes. "It probably sounds stupid, but I really love the way you laugh."

Flattered beyond measure, Lisa gave him a bright smile. "I've never heard anything less stupid in my life. Thank you."

Standing on tiptoe, she kissed his cheek. When she registered how smooth his skin felt, she gaped at him. "You shaved."

"Yeah." Running a hand over his face, he gave her a sheepish grin. "It was getting a little scruffy."

She hadn't taken a good look at him when they drove out together, just saw that he was wearing jeans and a jacket. Now she stepped back and gave him a thorough once-over. "Those are new jeans."

"Yeah."

She ticked the collar of his navy button-down, noticing how it deepened the color of his eyes. "And a shirt with a collar."

He shrugged, his face getting a little pinker than it had been. That this strong, courageous man could still blush simply amazed her. She'd invented a harsh back-story for him, and it didn't allow for humility. Somehow, despite what he'd been through, he'd kept hold of a boyishly soft heart. It was quite possibly the most endearing quality she'd ever seen in a man.

"Gus doesn't sell clothes like these at the hardware store," she pointed out.

"I went into town, and you were right." Grinning, he added, "Everything I needed was right there on Main Street."

If she didn't know better, she'd have thought he was flirting with her. She was just about to test her theory when Ridge came busting through the kitchen door with John close on his heels.

Matt pounded down the stairs, hair still wet from a shower. Like three clueless bulls in a china shop, they collapsed into chairs at the table and started fanning through the newspaper. Kyle and Emily came traipsing in from the living room, each of them talking over the other to get their father's attention. When Marianne reappeared with an armful of towels, in her mother-hen tone she ordered everyone to wash their hands before they ate. Ignoring their protests that their hands were perfectly clean, she turned away and carted the towels upstairs.

When Caty's MG convertible pulled into the driveway, Tucker went berserk until Kyle opened the door so the Lab could go greet their new arrival.

"Is it always like this?" Seth asked over the din.

Nodding, Lisa had to laugh. "Welcome to the Sawyer Farm."

* * *

Since the apartments above the diner were all empty except for his, Seth knew he wouldn't be bothering anyone if he got an early start Saturday morning. By seven, he'd finished laying the rest of the floorboards he'd been working on yesterday. The stain took him about an hour, and after that he couldn't do anything more until it dried.

Cutting planks for the other floor would create a lot of dust, so they'd have to wait. That meant he was free to go over to the church and get organized before folks started showing up. He buckled on his tool belt and went downstairs to grab something to eat before heading out.

With each step down, the noise from the dining room got louder and louder. It was so bad, he could barely hear the woman on the radio singing about rockin' around the Christmas tree. When he stopped in the kitchen, over the swinging doors he saw the diner jam-packed with the people he'd be seeing later on.

Good-natured arguments and laughter

came from every table. Several guys dressed head to toe in hunter's camouflage were even singing along with the music in very questionable voices. A few days ago, the thought of walking into all that chaos would have sent Seth running back upstairs.

Not today, though, he realized with a measure of pride. Now he knew some of his aunt's customers, and he spotted Pastor Charles sitting with three women. One of them was holding his hand loosely in a loving gesture Seth recognized from his own parents. Smiling, he strolled over to their table.

"Good morning," he said. "You're looking even better than yesterday, sir."

"Fit as ever," the preacher assured him. Motioning to the woman beside him, he added, "This is my wife, Penny."

Seth offered his hand. "Seth Hansen. It's a pleasure to meet you, ma'am."

To his surprise, she stood to embrace him. Beaming up at him as if he were some kind of celebrity she'd been dying to meet, she said, "I'm so glad you came over, Seth.

I've been wanting to thank you for rescuing Charlie."

She was so sincere, so obviously grateful, Seth forced himself not to blow off the praise. "I'm just glad I could help."

"God bless you."

The phrase made him want to squirm, and he covered his discomfort by turning to her husband. "Is Charles your first name or your last name?"

"Both," he replied with a chuckle. "My parents had an odd sense of humor."

"Won't you join us?" one of the other women asked. "I'm sure we can find a chair somewhere."

Seth really wasn't keen on the idea, since it would require him to come up with his share of polite conversation. Not his strong point. Still, he thought as he glanced around, if Lisa was here…

"She's off today," Penny told him.

Busted. When he looked at her, she gave him a knowing smile that made him laugh. "You've raised a son, I'm guessing."

"Four of them. You all think you're so

good at hiding what you're thinking, but you're wrong."

He grinned down at the woman who seemed like the perfect match to her husband. "You sound like my mom."

"Really? From the way you say it, I'll take that as a compliment."

"It is. Thanks for the invitation, but I'd best get over to the site before everyone finishes breakfast. The cleanup's almost done, and I'd like to start framing that wall on Monday."

"We'll be over later with coffee," one of the pastor's companions said.

"Sounds great. I'll see you then."

Waving, Seth headed out the door and across the street. As he approached the square, his discomfort grew with each step. Even though he'd been recruited by the man in charge, it didn't seem right that someone who'd turned away from God should be in charge of rebuilding a house of worship.

Seth tried regarding it the way Lisa had suggested, as a building. Cozy and unassuming, the little white church looked like many others he'd seen during his travels. It had been built simply, its only embellishments being a modest steeple and that unique stained-glass window. But he knew from his inspection yesterday that, old as they were, those walls had been built to last.

Even though he wasn't from Harland, he recognized that this chapel was part of the town's history, and it meant a lot to the people giving up their time to help make it whole again. People like Aunt Ruth and the Sawyers who were busy enough as it was but had offered their help without complaint.

They were like a family, he realized as he climbed the front steps. Working together to make Pastor Charles's promise of holding Christmas Eve service there a reality. In his memory, Lisa's voice rang as clearly as if she were standing right beside him.

I've gone to Christmas Eve service in that church every year since I was born. I can't imagine it any other way.

Seth wished he felt a connection like that

to a special place. Any place, he thought while he got his hard hat from a rack and pulled on his work gloves. He'd spent most of the past two years trying to forget all the cities and towns he'd been to, desperate to put those memories out of his mind so he could get on with his life.

Had it worked? Not so much, he admitted with a sigh. The problem was, he didn't know what else to do.

Taking a clipboard from its hook, he skimmed the checklist of jobs he'd made up for today. If they got through half of them, he'd be amazed, but he didn't see the point in setting the bar low. High expectations would motivate people to work more efficiently, he reasoned. When he realized that was one of his father's lessons, Seth grinned. The older he got, the smarter Dad seemed to be.

The first thing on his personal list was to build a box around the irreplaceable window. He gathered the materials he needed and started toward the front of the church. Building, he corrected himself, taking a deep breath to keep his nerves under control. This was a building that needed to be repaired, nothing more. He was good at that.

As he neared the front pews, the sunlight streaming through the remaining side windows broke through the gloom and made everything look more cheerful. Hopeful, almost. Distracted by the foolish thought, Seth cautioned himself to concentrate and set down the wood he was carrying. After measuring the opening, he tapped around to find some studs he could nail into without damaging the carved frame around the window.

He built the box on the floor and partially banged in some nails around the edges to make things easier when he lifted it into place later. He stood up, and a shaft of sunlight hit the colored glass just right, making it look like a million gems sparkling in the morning sun.

Deep golds, vivid blues and emerald greens glowed with what he could only describe as warmth. The slender gold halo over Jesus's head stood out from the background, and Seth noticed something he hadn't seen before.

A hammer.

By Jesus's bare feet lay an old wooden mallet like the kind carpenters used to use. Squinting, Seth looked for other tools disguised in the artwork and found a plane and a chisel. He wouldn't have seen them from a distance, and they were so cleverly integrated into the design he was sure most people wouldn't have spotted them even up close.

Seth found himself staring at the face depicted in the window. He didn't know what he expected, but he focused on it for a long time. The longer he looked, the warmer the colors seemed to get. Crazy as it seemed, he felt as if someone was trying to communicate with him. Thanking him for helping to restore the broken church back to the way it was meant to be.

Welcoming him home.

"Is everything okay?"

Seth spun toward her, and Lisa frowned at the spooked expression on his face. She'd been standing there long enough to worry about him gazing up at the church's signature window as if he was in some kind of trance. Now she was really concerned.

"Seth, you're white as a sheet." Hurrying toward the front of the aisle, she asked, "Are you okay?"

He nodded slowly, but his eyes cut to the animal scene again as if he thought it might have changed since he last saw it two seconds ago. She knew a lot of people who felt a special connection to the artwork, but she'd never seen anyone react to it the way he had. It was as if he'd found something disturbing in the old glass and was having a hard time putting it out of his mind.

"It's real pretty," he finally said, focusing on her with a wan smile. "How old is it?"

"As old as the church. Daniel Sawyer made it and hung it himself when they dedicated the chapel in 1860."

"That's why this place means so much to your family," Seth commented as the color came back into his face. "Did you get your talent for painting from him?"

She'd never really thought about it, but his question made her laugh. "Probably. Our family tree has a lot more farmers than artists."

"That just makes you special."

Genuine affection warmed his smile, making her *feel* special. "What a sweet thing to say. Thank you."

When he hunkered down, she noticed the wooden box on the floor near his feet. As she knelt beside him, she asked, "What's this for?"

"I want to cover the window so we don't wreck it while we're pulling things down and putting them back up."

"We're mostly just cleaning up today."

"I like to work ahead," he explained. "Keeps things moving along."

The meaning beneath his words hit her, and she smiled at him. "You're going to make sure this church is ready for Christmas Eve, aren't you?"

"That's what the pastor wants." He connected with her eyes in a rare direct gaze.

"And you. It's important to you, and I want you to have it."

"Why?" Realizing that sounded rude, she quickly added, "I mean, we hardly know each other. Why does it matter so much what I want?"

"You're a good person, and you deserve to be happy."

Determination lit his eyes, and Lisa had no doubt that if he had to work around the clock he'd make sure she wasn't disappointed. Knowing he thought so much of her sent a tingle of excitement racing down her spine. What would it be like to be the woman he loved? she wondered. Would he use his considerable will to make all her dreams come true?

While romantic notions were spinning through her head, the double doors banged open and several people entered. After the clang of them setting down their tool kits, she heard someone say, "First ones here, as usual."

"Yeah," another replied. "Where's our fearless leader?"

The others laughed, and not in a nice way. When they started ripping into Seth, she started to stand up and give them a piece of her mind. Frowning, Seth put a hand on her arm and shook his head. She stayed put, but she didn't like it. No one should be allowed to run someone else down like that. It just wasn't right.

One of them had the gall to complain, "I don't know what the pastor's thinking, bringing in a stranger to tell us how to fix our own church. Y'ask me, it's a real slap in the face to Carl Miller."

"Carl's not complaining," one of his friends said sternly. "Neither should you. This Hansen kid's been through a lot, and the last thing he needs is you making things tougher on him."

"How do we even know he can handle a crew like this?"

"He's military," a familiar voice told him in a measured tone. "That's good enough for me."

It was Gus Williams, and Lisa barely restrained herself from rushing out to hug him. Revered around town for his Marine service and tireless charity work, if anyone could convince them to give Seth a fair shake, Gus could.

"I got plenty of respect for you service boys," one of the whiners said. "But this kid's like a ghost. He can't handle a rowdy, inexperienced bunch of volunteers."

"He'll handle them fine," Gus assured him. "Meantime, I could use some extra hands unloading the lumber I've got out in my truck."

They all tramped out after him, and the doors slammed closed.

"Morons," Lisa seethed as she and Seth got to their feet. "You should have set them straight."

"Folks don't just give you respect," he explained patiently, as if she were a child who needed the lesson. "You have to earn it."

Still peeved, she tilted her chin defiantly up in the air. "I'd never let anyone talk about me like that."

"I don't doubt that for a second. But I don't make much of a first impression.

When they see what I can do, they'll change their minds about me."

He'd made an incredible first impression on her, but she wasn't about to tell him that. In her experience, praising a guy made him expect all kinds of things. Since Seth was going to be leaving town soon, she knew it was best to keep him at arm's length.

Too bad, she thought with a mental sigh. The more she saw of him, the more there was to like. Even if his extreme shifts in mood—from surfer-dude mellow to super-spy intense—did make her crazy.

Lisa angled a look over at Seth, expecting to see defeat in his eyes. Instead, they snapped with determination.

"Don't worry," he said as he lifted the box into place over the window. "I know more about building than they think."

"It would be hard not to."

They both laughed, and she held the box steady while he hammered it into place. When two of the judgmental idiots returned carting armloads of lumber, they stopped just inside the door and gaped at Seth and

Lisa. Apparently, they didn't mind trashing someone if they thought he wasn't listening, but being caught at it was embarrassing.

Feeling just snotty enough to be mean, she gave them the sugary smile she used on difficult customers who needed to be coerced into leaving her more than a quarter as a tip. "Hal, your wife asked me to let her know when we need those batches of chili the Ladies' Aid is making for the crew. Tell her tomorrow would be great."

"Sure," he mumbled, his face reddening by the second.

"And Gerry," she added in the same sugary tone, "anytime you want to bring those tables we're borrowing from the firehouse, you can set them up in the square."

"Will do, Lisa."

He exchanged an awkward look with his buddy, and they took off with their tails between their legs.

Turning back to Seth, she gave him a triumphant smile. "That's how you deal with narrow-minded fools."

She anticipated him making some kind of flip remark, but instead he fixed her with a serious look. "You didn't have to do that, but thanks."

"You're welcome."

When the noon fire whistle blew, everyone trooped outside for some fresh air. Parking an empty wheelbarrow he'd been using, Seth glanced around for Lisa and realized she wasn't there. He'd been so busy trucking debris out to the Dumpsters, he hadn't noticed when she'd left. More disappointed than he should have been, he put her out of his mind and got back to work.

The biggest stuff was gone, so he was down to shoveling smaller pieces into the wheelbarrow. He'd just come back from dumping his last load when someone tapped him on the shoulder. He turned to find Lisa behind him, holding a tray. The food was covered with metal covers, but he could smell something delicious steaming through the holes.

"Lunchtime."

She flashed him a bright smile before heading back down the aisle. Clearly, she meant for him to follow her.

"Thanks, but I'm good."

Turning, she nailed him with a give-me-a-break look. "You don't expect me to eat by myself, do you?"

This pretty lady seemed determined to make sure he didn't spend too much time on his own. He wasn't sure why she cared so much, especially since it was obvious he aggravated her on a regular basis.

Get a grip, he scolded himself. Lisa was a nice woman who was giving him a little extra attention. Most guys would kill to be in his place right now, and he should just go with it.

Pushing away his lingering discomfort, he stripped off his gloves and shoved them in the back pocket of his jeans. "Since you put it like that, I guess it's time for lunch."

"Good boy."

With a satisfied feminine smirk, she led him outside to a picnic table under a tree. They sat at one end across from each other, and the conversation at the other end stopped abruptly. Judging by their reaction to his presence, Seth assumed these were the doubters that had irritated Lisa earlier this morning. He couldn't help admiring her in-your-face attitude. It contradicted the accommodating, friendly personality she showed when she was waitressing. To him, the extra layer made her even more fascinating.

"Nice move," he murmured as she set their dishes on the table and stacked the trays.

"Mess with my friends," she hissed with a false smile. She didn't finish the threat, but he got the gist from the blue fury snapping in her eyes.

When her words registered more clearly, Seth asked, "You consider us friends?"

"Definitely," she assured him breezily while she unwrapped her club sandwich. "Don't you?"

Smiling, he unrolled his napkin and took out his silverware. "I guess I do."

"You're trying to figure out when it happened, aren't you?"

A few days ago, her uncanny ability to guess his thoughts would have sent him into a panic. Now, it made him laugh. Maybe he was actually making progress.

"You're pretty good at that mind-reading thing."

Lifting the cover from his food, he found a deep bowl full of his aunt's Irish stew. As he glanced around, he noticed that everyone else had sandwiches. "Thanks again."

"I figured since you're the head guy, you should get something special for lunch."

Smiling, she patted his left arm. It was the one that still gave him trouble, and he ignored it as much as possible. Even though it had healed well, he couldn't look at the scars in the mirror. Lisa had seen them, though, and he couldn't believe she wanted to touch him at all. Most people would be horrified, but he was beginning to understand she wasn't like most people. That thought led him back to the way she'd dealt with Hal and Gerry. Without hesitation, she'd made it very clear that she knew what they'd said about Seth and wouldn't stand for any more nonsense.

You didn't encounter that kind of integrity very often. It reminded Seth of how the men in his unit had looked out for each other, even when all their backs were up against a wall. The last place he'd expect to find that kind of backbone was in a bubbly country girl who'd taught herself to paint. Maybe Aunt Ruth was right. It seemed there was a lot more to Lisa Sawyer than blue eyes and a gorgeous smile.

Swallowing around the sudden lump in his throat, he forced himself to meet her eyes directly. "You probably hate secrets."

"Pretty much."

"I can't do anything about that. I'm sorry."

With an unreadable expression, she studied him for what felt like forever. Hard as he tried, Seth couldn't make himself look away. Shifting emotions swirled through her eyes: compassion, confusion, concern. The one that amazed him most was something he'd assumed he'd never see again.

Acceptance.

Tilting her head, she popped a slice of pickle into her mouth. "So what you're saying is if we're going to be friends, I have to take you as is, without asking a lot of questions you can't answer."

Hearing it put so bluntly made it sound downright rude, but she had the basic idea, so he nodded. "Yeah."

"You didn't look away this time." Giving him an encouraging smile, she patted his arm again. "I must be growing on you."

Big-time. Since he didn't want to scare her by coming across as needy, Seth settled for a quick grin. "Maybe."

She laughed. "Seth Hansen, are you flirting with me?"

"Maybe." Inspiration struck, and he added, "Is it working?"

She regarded him with a tilt of her head. "Did you get that from a movie?"

"Yeah." Feeling the heat in his face, he knew he looked like a total idiot. "Flirting's not my strong point."

"That's okay. You've got lots of other

strong points that are way more interesting."

Her open, honest approval of him left Seth totally at a loss. When he noticed her staring over his shoulder, he asked, "Something wrong?"

"I know it sounds stupid, but I'll really miss that old tree. Everything changes, I guess," she added with a wistful sigh.

She sounded so sad, he wished there was something he could do to bring that tree back for her. Since that was impossible, he tried to find reassuring words. Before he could come up with something intelligent to say, a man bellowed Lisa's name, and she got up from her seat.

"Duty calls," she said as she slid an order pad from the back pocket of her jeans. "See you later?"

When Seth realized it was a question, his brain kicked his mouth into gear. "Sure. I'll be around."

She left him with a warm parting smile and moved around the tables, taking orders for extra sandwiches and more drinks.

Watching her chatting and laughing with the volunteers, Seth realized she hadn't finished her own lunch. Instead, she'd spent her precious free time making him feel more at ease, bolstering his confidence to the point where he felt as though he could tackle anything this project—and his crew— threw at him.

He just wished there was something he could do for her in return. When an idea flashed into his mind, it actually made him smile.

Chapter Seven

When she got back from the church site late Saturday afternoon, Lisa looked around her apartment and groaned. The dust had gotten way out of hand, but she really hated cleaning. Marianne was ruthlessly neat, and when they were sharing a room growing up, Lisa had gone the other way out of spite. She knew where everything was. Everything important, anyway. It wasn't hard to keep track of stuff in a studio apartment.

Right now, the most important thing was Cleo's laser pointer. One of the coolest cat toys ever invented, it shined a pinpoint red dot on whatever you aimed it at. Cleo went bonkers chasing it, and it was great exercise for her, but Lisa couldn't find the silly thing.

Looking peeved, the Maine coon was sitting regally in the middle of the living-room floor with her bushy tail curled around her paws. Her expression clearly said, "What's wrong with you?"

"I know, I know," Lisa muttered as she lay down on the floor to look under the furniture. "I'll find it."

When someone knocked on the door, she was so annoyed she just yelled, "Come in!"

From behind, she heard a now-familiar voice. "Lose something?"

Rolling onto her side, she looked up at Seth. "My mind. Cleo's favorite toy is missing."

"Aww, that's too bad." Hunkering down, he held a hand out toward the cat. She promptly abandoned Lisa and went to give Seth her version of a hug. Rubbing her cheek on his jeans, she purred sweetly at him.

"Traitor," Lisa scolded with a laugh. "It looks like she's got a new favorite toy."

"I'm honored, your highness." Grinning, he stood and offered Lisa a hand up. "I'm actually here to see you, though."

Hearing that made her foolish heart skip like a little girl with a jump rope. They were just friends, she reminded herself as she stood to face him. "Really? What for?"

He nodded at the pile of language books still sitting—unopened—on the counter. "You're not gonna learn anything from them." Then he motioned to the framed print of the Eiffel Tower hanging on her living-room wall. "It occurred to me you're a visual person. If you had pictures, it'd be easier to learn the words."

"Like a kid's picture book of Europe or something?"

"I've got something even better than that."

Sliding his phone from the front pocket of his frayed jeans, he scrolled to something and handed it to her. It was a beautiful shot of the famous tower, only it was lit from behind by the rising sun. The rays glinted off the steel, making it look as if it were made of gold.

"That's the most beautiful thing I've ever seen," she breathed in amazement. Staring up at him, she asked, "Did you take this picture?"

"Well, no. I didn't have much time for sightseeing, but a buddy of mine visited all the places you're interested in. I had him send me some of his best shots for you to look at. I thought if we went through them, you could describe them to me. Then I could tell you how to say the same thing in French or Italian or whatever."

Impressed by his creativity, she nodded eagerly. "That's a fabulous idea. When can we start?"

"How 'bout now?"

If she'd learned anything about Seth, it was that he was the least impulsive person on the planet. He thought things through carefully, weighing his options before deciding what to do. In his eyes, she saw a shadow of his characteristic hesitation, and she realized he wasn't sure she'd like his suggestion.

To chase off any lingering doubts, she gave him her brightest smile. "Now is perfect. Would you like a snack or something?"

He cracked an irresistible little boy's grin. "On my way up I thought I smelled gingerbread."

"Would you like milk with that?"

"Sure. Thanks."

She stacked some of Marianne's yummy gingerbread men on a plate and poured two glasses of milk to go with them. After joining him on the sofa, she picked up a cookie and pointed to the caption on her poster. "*La Tour Eiffel.* I know that much, anyway."

"*Très bien.*"

"That means 'very good,' right?"

"*Oui.* See? You're doing great."

"That's movie French," she scoffed. "Anybody can do that."

"You've got a nice accent, though. The worst thing you can do is speak French like an American. They'll peg you as a tourist in a heartbeat." He handed over his phone. *"Allons-y."*

"What?"

"It means 'let's go.'"

She laughed. "Got it."

While they munched their cookies, she scrolled through the "France" album on his phone. As she stopped at each picture, he told her what it was and had her describe it in English. After he translated what she'd said into French, he broke down each phrase so she could repeat it. Once they'd gone through ten of them, he took her back to the beginning to see what she remembered.

To her astonishment, she recalled most of the descriptions with only a slight nudge from him here and there.

"Great job," he approved with a grin. "You learn fast. Must be all that practice keeping people's favorite orders straight."

His praise made her squirm a little. School wasn't her thing, and she'd barely gotten through some of her classes. Marianne was the brain, and Lisa was—what?

The pretty one? No, her big sister was absolutely beautiful. The friendly one? No, that was John. Matt defied classification, so she guessed that made him the mysterious one.

Where did that leave her? She'd never really thought about it, and now that she had, it was more than a little sobering. She was just Lisa, the baby. Maybe that was why everyone treated her like one. Everyone but Seth, that was. He made her feel like a grown-up, admiring her artwork, making friends with her cat. It was a new experience for her, and she liked it.

"You're a really great teacher." Finishing off her milk, she asked, "How did you learn all this?"

When he looked down, she backpedaled like a left fielder. "I'm sorry, Seth. I guess I'm curious by nature. Kind of like Cleo." She smiled, hoping to ease the sudden awkwardness her innocent question had caused.

"That's okay. I know I'm not like most folks you've met."

Thank God for that, she thought. To him,

she said, "No, but being like everyone else is so overrated."

He angled a doubtful glance at her, but she didn't let that derail her. Instead, she smiled back and took their dishes into the kitchen. "Want some more?"

"Sure."

"I have to confess, these are my sister's cookies. She and the kids made too many, so I lucked out." As she returned with his refill, she added, "I didn't want you thinking I'm domestic or anything."

A slow grin spread across his chiseled features, and the ice in his eyes warmed to a pale blue. "Good to know." Glancing toward the easel, he squinted and got up for a closer look.

"You're making great progress on this. The background looks so real, it's like I could just step right in and grab a piece of chicken out of the picnic basket."

"Thank you."

That he even remembered how the painting had looked earlier in the week simply floored her. For him to notice the changes she'd made, he must have a real eye for detail.

Turning to her, he asked, "Was this picnic at the church? Under the tree you said you were going to miss?"

"Yes, it was."

"The one the landscaper shredded and chipped down to the ground today." Looking back at the painting, he shook his head. "That's a real shame. It was a beautiful tree."

The honest emotion in his voice touched her in a surprising way. There was definitely more to this carpenter than met the eye. Normally, she went for sweet, simple guys who adored her but didn't have much in the way of depth.

Seth was another animal altogether. Even though she usually shied away from dark and mysterious, she couldn't help being fascinated by the past he couldn't share with her. What had happened to make him the way he was now? He hadn't told her much about himself, but she'd pieced together a sketchy history on her own. Given enough time, she could probably figure him out enough to truly appreciate him.

Not that she wanted to, she cautioned herself. The woman who took him on with all his shadowy baggage would have to be endlessly patient with him. While she believed in her heart that he was worth the effort, Lisa recognized that she was better off being his friend. Since they'd be working together on the church in addition to him tutoring her, they'd be spending a lot of time together. Keeping this baffling man at a respectable distance was the smart thing to do.

So why did she suddenly feel sad?

Sunday morning, Seth added two more folding chairs to the rows set out in the empty diner. After stacking and shoving all the tables against the walls, he'd been helping his aunt set out row after row of chairs borrowed from the Harland Rotary Club.

"That's the last of them," he finally said.

"Hmm." Tapping her finger in the air, she counted. "We need a couple right here for the Simmons family. Their son and daughter-in-law are in town this weekend, and they'll want to sit together during the service."

Seth could see where this was going, and he tried to nip her rearranging in the bud. "You're kidding. Can't they sit behind them?"

She looked at him as if he'd suggested making them plunk down out on the sidewalk, and he sighed. "Fine. I'll move 'em."

"Thank you. And thank you for bringing the lectern over from the church," she added while he shifted the chairs. "It makes things look a little more normal."

Glancing at the hand-carved oak stand, then around the diner all decked out for Christmas, he chuckled and shook his head. "Normal for Harland, anyway. This place is something else."

"Isn't it, though? The people here are so interesting, I can't imagine living anywhere else."

He couldn't miss the nudge in her voice, and he frowned at her. "Will you stop already? I know what you're doing, and you're wasting your time. Nothing's gonna happen between me and Lisa Sawyer."

"Really?" Her eyes narrowed in a you-can't-fool-me stare. "You've only been here a week, and you've been at her place more than your own."

"Helping out, is all."

"Helping how?"

He wasn't used to people nosing into his business, and it didn't thrill him now. As he considered how to answer, he reminded himself that she meant well, misplaced as her interest was. "Last night I started teaching her some French."

Arching a brow, Aunt Ruth grinned at him as if he'd said he'd gotten down on one knee and asked the lady to marry him. "Teaching her French is helping?"

"Someone has to make sure she doesn't get in trouble over there. She asked me to tutor her, and I agreed."

"After a fight, no doubt."

Unable to help himself, Seth grinned at

the memory. "There was a little scuffle at first. In the end, I did it to make her happy."

His aunt laughed. "She gets a lot of things that way."

"Doesn't surprise me in the least," he grumbled.

"So stubborn." Aunt Ruth came forward, stopping just short of where he stood. "So is she whenever I casually mention you. I wonder why."

Seth hated to think how often his aunt "casually" worked him into conversations with her goddaughter. Then again, it was nice to hear Lisa didn't appreciate it, either. "Maybe 'cause we don't like being shoved together by a meddling woman who doesn't know when to back off."

"Or maybe," she suggested without blinking, "you like each other and are just too mule headed to admit it."

He laughed at that. "Lisa doesn't strike me as the type to keep her opinions to herself. If she liked me, I don't think she'd have a problem telling you about it."

"And if you liked her, you'd be fine admitting it?"

Seth shrugged. "Sure."

"So you don't like her."

She pinned him with a stern look, and he started squirming like a ten-year-old. "Well, I didn't say that. She's real nice."

"And pretty, too."

"I guess."

"You guess?" she teased with a smug look. "She's gorgeous, and you know it. Of course, that's nothing compared to everything else she's got going for her. Being talented and funny and all," she added as if he needed a map.

Resting his hands on the back of a chair, Seth picked at the remnant of a price tag so she couldn't see just how interested he was in Lisa. "Girls like her don't go for guys like me."

When Aunt Ruth hummed, he glanced up to find her smiling at him. "Seth, do you remember when you were eight, and you wanted that new bike?"

"Sure."

"But you didn't tell your parents because your father was out of work and money was so tight?"

"Yeah. You showed up Christmas morning with it in the back of your van."

Stepping closer, she put a reassuring hand on the shoulder that would never completely heal. "I got you that bike because you were a good boy and never asked for anything. I thought you deserved to have something that would make you happy. You're all grown-up now, but you still deserve that."

"Women aren't like bikes," he argued. "You can't just wrap one up and give her to me."

"I can try," she insisted with a fond smile. "The choice is yours, but I pray you'll decide to take a chance someday. If not with Lisa, then someone else. You're a good man, and there's no reason on God's earth you shouldn't be happy."

He knew she meant for her talk of praying for him to make him feel better somehow. Instead, it made him edgy, and Seth gently pulled away. "I'd best get out of here before folks start showing up."

"You could join us if you want."

He glanced at the oak lectern with its hand-carved cross and barely suppressed a shudder. "No, thanks. I'm headed over to the church to see where we should start tomorrow morning. That wall's not going to frame itself."

She shrugged, but he could tell she wasn't pleased. As much as he hated to disappoint her, this time he couldn't do what she wanted without feeling like a hypocrite.

"Suit yourself," she said. "If you want lunch, things should be ready about noon."

"Maybe," he hedged, trying it out to see how it felt. Still not totally comfortable, but it didn't make him want to run off, either. It seemed he was finally making some real progress, he mused with a grin. "Sounds good, actually."

"Good," she replied as she opened the door for him. "I'll see you then."

As he passed by, he paused and smiled down at her. "Thanks, Auntie."

"For what?"

She knew what he meant, which was a good thing since he had no idea how to express it. Trusting her to understand, he leaned down to kiss her cheek on his way out. Beaming her approval, she ruffled his hair and waved him away.

"Get outta here, now. I've got people coming."

Feeling better than he had in a long, long time, he strolled across the street, whistling "Deck the Halls" as he went.

Lisa did her best to focus on the service that morning, but nothing she did could keep her mind from wandering. To make matters worse, her eyes kept drifting to the front window that looked out toward the town square and its quaint collection of churches. Several times, she caught a glimpse of Seth going down the makeshift side ramp with a wheelbarrow, headed to the Dumpster.

He hadn't been at the diner when she arrived with her family, so she knew he'd been at the work site for at least an hour, cleaning up the last of the plaster and splintered wood. It didn't take much imagination for her to picture him over there, his hair and clothes dusty from sweeping. All alone, no radio or anything, the way he worked on the apartments upstairs. The way he did everything, it seemed.

Because, as Ruthy had confided, he'd lost his faith in everything he once believed in. Knowing that about him made Lisa incredibly sad. It was so hard to weather the nasty turns in life without God to lean on. No matter how strong someone was, God was stronger.

When Marianne nudged her shoulder, Lisa glanced over and got The Eye. With a muted sigh, she turned forward and tried—again—to pay attention to Pastor Charles. The bandage above his eye was smaller today, and he beamed like a man who wouldn't want to be anywhere else this morning.

Lisa wished she shared his contentment with where she was and what she was doing. Something was bothering her, but she hadn't been able to pin it down. She'd made the deposit on her European tour package yesterday, so it was just a matter of time before she'd be going. It wasn't an "if" anymore, it was a "when." She'd even started crossing out the days between now and then on her calendar.

She should have been thrilled, but the anticipation felt oddly hollow, as if something was missing from her plans. Unfortunately, she had no clue what it could be, and that only made her edgier about the whole thing.

She'd dreamed about it for so long, maybe she'd built it up too much. Or maybe she should add something to the itinerary, or spend more time in Paris, or…

"Earth to Lisa."

Jerked out of her thoughts by John's voice, she noticed the service was over and everyone around her was getting to their feet. Feeling more than a little foolish, she got up and tried to think of a good excuse for flaking out in the middle of a sermon.

"Sorry. I guess I was a little distracted."

"Seth's all by himself over there," Marianne said with a smile. "Why don't you go see if he needs a hand?"

"That's not what's distracting me."

As if on cue, her brothers broke up laughing, and she caught Ridge contorting a grin into something slightly less insulting.

"It's *not,*" she insisted more forcefully. "I was thinking about where to go during my trip."

"Sure you were," John taunted with one of his maddening grins. "Isn't all that set in stone by the tour company?"

Huffing, she glared up at him. "I have time where I can do things on my own. I'm trying to decide what to see."

"Whatever." Still grinning like a moron, he fell in line behind Matt and Caty. Over his shoulder, he made a kissy face at Lisa.

"Oh, grow up," she shot back, mimicking the gesture. "You look like a trout."

The three guys laughed at her on their way out, and she rolled her eyes.

"Don't mind them, honey," a very pregnant Caty advised. "They've been working like crazy all week, and they need some entertainment."

Lisa gave a very unladylike snort. "Well, if they start up again at lunch, I'm leaving."

"Oh, don't tell them that," Marianne cautioned while she helped Emily with the top button on her pink coat. "They'll never stop."

"Boys are so stupid," Emily chimed in, and the girls all laughed as they filed down the makeshift aisle.

When they were outside, Lisa looked over at the church and saw Seth sprawled on the front steps, drinking a bottle of water. As he leaned forward, he rested his elbows on his knees and dangled the water bottle between them as he stared at the ground.

"He looks exhausted."

The others stared at her, and Lisa realized she'd spoken out loud. It was too late to wiggle her way out of this one, so she didn't even try. "I think I'll go see if I can get him to take a break."

"Invite him to lunch," Marianne suggested as Ridge opened the passenger door of their minivan for her. "We've got plenty of ham to go around."

"Thanks," Lisa replied. "I will."

Careful to avoid cars pulling away from the curb, she crossed the street and walked toward where Seth was sitting. Before she was even halfway there, he was on his feet and brushing himself off. She smiled as she reached the steps. "Good morning."

"Same to you," he responded with a shy smile. "How was your service?"

"A little strange, but nice. It was nice of you to help Ruthy set everything up."

Wiping his hands on the bandanna he always carried in his back pocket, he shrugged as if it was nothing. "Once everyone clears out, I'll go reset for lunch."

"I'll help you," she offered without thinking. When he gave her a funny look, she explained, "It'll go faster that way."

"Don't you have a family meal to get to?"

"They can wait. My brothers just torture me the whole time, anyway."

"Yeah," he said with a sheepish grin. "My sisters used to do the same thing to me."

"They don't live near your parents anymore?"

"No, they're around. They just don't torture me anymore."

"I'm confused," Lisa confessed. "Why the change?"

Sighing, he folded his handkerchief into a neat square and slid it back into his jeans. "Everything changed."

Translation: after he came home in pieces, his sisters didn't want to make things worse by teasing him. They couldn't possibly have known that by being extra nice, they'd actually made him feel worse.

Trying to shift the conversation to something positive, she asked, "Are they all older than you?"

"Yeah."

"It's the worst, right?" When he glanced up with some interest, she rattled on. "I mean, everyone thinks you've got it made, being the youngest. Grown-ups spoil you, and older brothers and sisters look out for you. Then later on, they can't get used to the fact that you're all grown-up, and they still treat you like a baby."

She was keenly aware she sounded like a babbling idiot, but the misery had left Seth's eyes, and he grinned. "That's how it is, all right."

"And Ruthy's the worst," she added, shaking her head with a smile. "She mothers everyone she meets, which is really sweet, and I love her for it. But sometimes she forgets we're not ten anymore."

Seth laughed, and Lisa applauded herself for dragging him out of the funk she'd inadvertently created. It had been an innocent question, but she still felt bad for bringing up sad memories.

"Speaking of Aunt Ruth, I should get back there. Sure you want to help?"

"Mais oui," she replied, linking her arm through his. *"Allons-y."*

Laughing again, he nodded his approval as they walked through the square. *"Très bien, mademoiselle."*

"Merci beaucoup."

By the time they got to the diner, Lisa had exhausted her very limited French vocabulary. But Seth was smiling, and she considered that a major success.

Chapter Eight

Monday morning, Seth arrived at the church work site around seven. There were a few things to do before they could start framing, and he figured they'd go quicker if he did them himself. After the grumbling he'd overheard, he expected some pushback from at least a couple of the volunteers. While he'd never shrunk from a fight, it wasn't his style to seek one out, either.

As if destroying the century-old tree wasn't bad enough, the storm had thoroughly soaked the raised altar area. It was basically a simple stage, but he went over it carefully, stomping on the steps and platform to test the strength of the remaining wood. Still damp in spots, it gave in several places, and the splintering sounds he heard didn't bode well for the supports underneath. He pulled a couple of face boards away and discovered that the structure, solid as it may have been in 1860, was far from sturdy now.

The best option was to pull it all out and rebuild it. No big deal, he thought, until he turned his attention to the damaged oak pews. The lumber had come from the forests around Harland, Gus had told him. Replacing the wood was no problem, but Seth feared matching the layers of different stains would be impossible. He could never mix the right color of brown in a million years. Michelangelo, maybe. Seth, not a chance.

Lisa.

Her name popped into his head with a suddenness that startled him. Crazy or not, he recognized that his subconscious had hit on the perfect solution to his aesthetic problem. With her artist's eye for color, he had no doubt Lisa could come up with the stain he needed to blend his newly built pieces in with the old ones.

Pleased with the idea, he pulled out his phone and added a note to ask her about it. Then he tucked the phone away and grabbed a crowbar to start pulling the stage apart.

"What do you think you're doing?"

Seth recognized one of the complaining voices he'd heard the other day and looked up to find a fiftyish man in jeans and a flannel shirt glaring down at him. Arms folded, he looked ready to yank the tool from Seth's hands and beat him with it.

Taking a quiet breath to settle his nerves, Seth stood and met the man's anger head-on. "This wood is too saturated to be safe. It needs to be replaced."

"Who told you that?"

"I did." Hoping he looked friendly, Seth offered his hand. "Seth Hansen."

"I know who you are," the man shot back, eyes narrowed. "I just don't know why you think you can start ripping our church apart without asking first."

His claim to the church explained some of his bitterness toward Seth. It was understandable that a member of the close-knit congregation would feel that someone who belonged there should be the one in charge.

"I'm not," Seth explained. "Pastor Charles asked me to look at the interior structure and replace anything the storm damaged. I'm just following orders, sir."

Mentioning the pastor seemed to reassure the guy a little. He was still frowning, but he nodded. "That's all right, I guess."

Since the ice wasn't quite as slick as it had been, Seth took a shot. "I didn't catch your name, sir."

"I didn't throw it at you." The man backed away a few steps, all the while scowling at Seth. "I've worshipped in this church my whole life, never missed a single Sunday. I think it's wrong to trust it to some yahoo who can't spend a little time in God's house on the Sabbath."

This guy was a complete jerk who knew absolutely nothing about Seth, so he almost let the condemning barb pass. But somewhere inside him, an old feeling rustled to life, standing up straight and proud.

"Your whole life, huh?" he challenged. "Too bad it doesn't show."

His mouth dropping open, his adversary stared at Seth as if he had three heads. "You'd best watch your step, junior. You don't want to make an enemy out of me."

"I'll keep that in mind." Just for good measure, he added, "Sir."

Turning on the heel of his steel-toed work boot, the grumbler stalked back the way he'd come. Unfortunately, Seth had known men like him, so stiff and cold they were like walking corpses. Sometimes he could get through to them, discover they had something in common so they could talk a little. Sometimes not. But he could work with anybody, and he had a feeling that over the next couple of weeks, that skill was going to come in very handy.

From the gaping hole in the wall, he heard muted laughter and looked over to find Gus grinning in at him.

"Nice shot, son."

"Thanks." Seth shook his head. "This is gonna be all over town by noon. I should've just let it go."

"Jim Canfield is a class-A mule when he gets a mind to be," Gus told him.

"I think I saw his truck out front. Canfield Roofing, right?"

"That's him. Great with plywood and shingles, lousy with people. I heard the whole thing, and you gave him exactly what he deserved."

Strolling over, Seth rested a hand near the opening. "Spying on me?"

Gus replied with an unapologetic grin. "You're doing good here, Seth. Just keep on the way you're going, and you'll be fine."

Seth got the feeling Gus was referring to more than his run-in with their prickly roofer. For some reason, the old Marine's approval made him feel prouder than he had in a long time. "I'll do that, sir."

"And quit calling me 'sir.' You're making me feel about a hundred years old."

That reminded him of Aunt Ruth griping

when people called her "ma'am," and Seth laughed. "Got it."

"I've got a big load of clapboard siding out there. Gimme a hand, would you?"

"Sure."

After clapping Seth on the shoulder, Gus led him out to a beautifully restored Model-T delivery truck with *Harland Hardware* painted on the side. A couple of volunteers introduced themselves to Seth and joined in to help. Before long, the truck was empty and Seth knew two more people than he did yesterday.

For most folks, shaking two new hands would have been no big deal. For Seth, it represented solid progress. Maybe, finally, he was wrestling his life back onto the right track.

"Whew!" Lisa dropped onto a stool at the counter, giving Ruthy what she knew was a pitiful look. "What is with people today? It hasn't stopped since seven."

"Everyone's in town doing their Christmas shopping," Ruthy answered while she topped off a pitcher with the delicious homemade maple syrup a local farm had started selling to the diner. "It's great for business."

"But tough on my feet," Lisa complained.

"The church project is keeping us busier than usual, with people coming in here to eat after their shifts. But if we're going to finish by Christmas Eve, we need all the hands we can get."

"Oh, it'll be done," Lisa assured her while she pulled her tips out of her apron pocket. "Seth promised me."

Preoccupied with sorting out the ones so she could cash them in for larger bills, it took her a minute to notice that Ruthy was uncharacteristically quiet. When she glanced up, she found her boss studying her with a slight smile.

At first Lisa was confused, then it dawned on her that she'd basically blurted out that Seth was hurrying the project along as a personal favor to her. Realizing she'd given Ruthy hope for them getting together, Lisa groaned. "Oh, no. I didn't mean it that way."

"Which way is that?"

"Don't try that clueless act on me." She tapped her chest. "I invented it. You've got that 'cat in cream, my plan is working perfectly' look."

"I don't know where you and Seth get the idea I'm trying to throw you together." Holding up her hands, she glanced around the humming dining room. "Like I don't have enough to do."

"Gee, I don't know. Maybe it was the mistletoe stunt."

She waved that away as if it was an annoying gnat. "Tradition, that's all. I offered to take another picture, but you told me not to."

"I just wanted the two of you to quit arguing." Ruthy tilted her head with a dubious look, and Lisa laughed. "Besides, it was a nice picture."

"I've had at least a hundred compliments on it while it's been hanging by the door. Seeing two gorgeous kids under the mistletoe makes people smile."

Now that she was grown-up, being called

a "kid" bugged Lisa to no end. Because she adored this woman, she pushed down her annoyance and ignored the comment. "You mean it makes them think they can find someone to stand under the mistletoe with, too."

"And what's wrong with that?" Ruthy planted her hands on her hips with a stern expression. "Lonely folks searching for someone to share their lives with could do with a little hope, don't you think?"

Recognizing that she'd struck a very personal nerve, Lisa backpedaled like crazy. "I guess I didn't think of it that way. I'm sorry."

She was sorry about more than her careless attitude, but Lisa wasn't sure how to say so without insulting the woman who'd done so much to fill the void left by her own mother. Ruth Benton, with her eight sons and twenty-four-and-a-half grandchildren, lived her life surrounded by people who adored her.

But every night, she went home to her big, elegant Victorian house alone. Lisa's studio wasn't anywhere near as grand, but her life was very similar. When she wasn't at the farm with her rowdy, loving family, her only consistent company was a cat who considered it her mission in life to make it into the *Guinness Book of World Records* for "Most Sleeping Done By Cat."

There was more out there for her, Lisa knew, but it didn't exist in Harland. She'd lived there her entire life and hadn't found it yet. Maybe it was in Europe. Or Australia, she mused for the first time. Last night on the Travel Channel, she'd watched a two-hour tour of the fascinating country. From cosmopolitan Sydney to the rugged outback, the diversity had mesmerized her to the point that she forgot to eat supper.

How much would an Aussie tour cost? she wondered. Maybe next winter, when it was summer in that part of the world, she'd go there and see it all for herself.

"Lisa."

Ruthy's sharp tone jerked her back to reality. "Yes?"

"You were a million miles away just

now," she said more gently. "Where do you go when you do that?"

Feeling more than a little foolish, Lisa sighed. "Australia. I wonder how long it takes to get there."

"Twenty hours." Settling onto the stool beside her, Seth laid a piece of wood on the counter and grimaced. "Besides that, they're fourteen hours ahead of us time-wise, so it's already tomorrow when you land. Takes a few days to get adjusted."

"You've been to Australia?" She realized she must sound like an idiot, but she couldn't get her head around the idea. It was tough for her to tamp down the spark of jealousy that flared up, but she knew it was wrong to feel that way so she did her best. "Is there any place I want to go you haven't been to already?"

Sipping the coffee his aunt had put in front of him, he shrugged. "I've never been to Iceland."

"Brrr." Lisa shivered. "Like anyone would even want to go there."

"Actually, it's supposed to be a great spot.

When the Vikings discovered it, they gave it that name to keep people away." He grinned. "Greenland's weather is a lot worse, and they called it the opposite on purpose."

"Clever Vikings," Lisa murmured.

"Yeah. Speaking of clever," he added, picking up the wood, "I need your help with something."

Her heart did one of its crazy little flips, and she waited a moment before saying anything. "I'm not good with saws and stuff."

Chuckling, he shook his head. "What I need is this color." He held up the worn plank for her to see. "When I make the new risers and pews, I'll stain them and spruce up the old ones. But first, the new wood needs to be this color."

"Otherwise, the new pieces will be lighter, even if you use the same stain."

"Bingo. So, I need an artist."

"And you thought of me?"

When he nodded, she saw he was completely serious. No one had ever called her an artist, even in teasing. Seth was treating her like a pro, asking for help from someone he considered an expert. It was flattering and more than a little intimidating.

Picking out accessories for the apartments had been easy and fun. Working on permanent fixtures for the church she loved would be much more demanding, not to mention stressful. If she messed up, everyone would know. Then again, if she nailed it, everyone would know that, too. They'd finally be forced to admit that ditzy, dreamy Lisa had something more to offer than a menu and a quick smile. This was her chance, she realized. And Seth was giving it to her.

"I refinished a table for Matt and Caty a while back, and I still have sample cans of some different stains at my place," she said before she could talk herself out of it. "My shift is over, so we can go now if you want."

"Great. *Allons-y.*"

They both laughed at their French inside joke, and he waited while she cashed in her tips and got her coat from the storeroom.

Then there they were, standing together under the mistletoe again.

Several heads turned, and she rolled her eyes. "Nosy."

A mischievous gleam lit Seth's eyes, and it struck her that it was the first time she'd seen that from him. Intensity and vulnerability she'd noticed many times, but never anything even remotely playful. She had to admit she liked it.

"We could give 'em something to talk about," he suggested in a conspiratorial murmur.

She giggled because it was all so ridiculous. "Sure. Why not?"

"Hey, Lisa," he said loudly, grinning at her. "We're under the mistletoe."

Feigning surprise, she looked up, then cocked her head at him. "Well, are you gonna kiss me or not?"

She was anticipating a quick peck like the one he'd given her before. Instead, he wrapped his arms around her and pulled her up off her feet into a luxurious kiss that lasted long enough to leave her out of breath. Warm and gentle, the softness of it amazed her. The effect was more stunning than if he'd backed her up against the wall and given her the kind of hard, demanding kiss she was accustomed to from other guys.

Lisa found herself sinking into it, relishing the feel of being circled in those strong arms. Her mind flashed back to the day he'd put himself between her and the storm, ignoring his own safety to protect her. This was a man meant for keeping, a voice in her head warned. Not the kind of guy she wanted in her life right now.

Or was he?

Flustered, she pulled away and stared up at him. Most males on the planet would have been smug, but Seth was wearing an expression that must have mirrored hers. His bewildered look told her he'd felt the same rush of emotions she had when they kissed.

And it scared him, too.

In an effort to lighten the mood, she

forced a laugh and patted his chest. "Nice one."

Always the gentleman, he went around her to open the door, then stood back to hold it open. Feeling a little steadier now, she managed a shaky smile. "Thank you."

"For the door or the kiss?"

His tone was light, as hers had been, but there was an uncertainty in his eyes that made her heart twist a little tighter around this baffling contradiction of a man. Instinct told her this wasn't a time for teasing him, and she smiled back. "Both."

"That's good," he said as they headed down the sidewalk. "I wasn't sure how it was. I'm a little out of practice."

"You could've fooled me," she blurted without thinking. When he didn't respond, she tried to smooth over her impulsive comment. "It must've been the mistletoe."

"Yeah, that's it. Rotten weed."

Was he serious, or was he covering up some unintentional hurt feelings? She chanced a look over at him, but he was checking out the store windows as they passed by, so she couldn't see his face. It didn't really matter, she consoled herself. She'd settled on being friends with him, and no matter how mind-boggling their first real kiss had been, she knew the smartest approach was to stick with her plan.

Too bad she hadn't realized how tough that would be, she thought as they climbed the stairs to her apartment. From his solid work ethic to his soft heart, Seth was proving himself to be the kind of guy who could change her mind about that total-independence thing.

It didn't matter, she told herself for the thousandth time. The trouble was, somewhere along the line, the mantra she'd been using to keep him at bay had lost some of its power. While it was still true that he'd be going home soon and she'd be in Europe, a budding idea was beginning to push its way from the back of her mind to the front.

There could be a way to blend their plans into something that suited them both. She enjoyed his company, and he seemed to enjoy hers. Sought it out, actually, as he had with this color-matching project. Was it because she was the first friend he'd made in Harland and he was leaning on her, or was there something more to it?

Still mulling that over, she unlocked her door. When she stepped inside, she was surprised that Cleo wasn't there to greet her. It was past lunchtime, and her furry roommate should have been sitting by the door, looking perturbed at having to wait for her meal.

"Cleo?"

Nothing. She called out again with the same result, and a quick scan of the single room showed her the cat wasn't in any of her usual napping spots.

"You think she found another way out?" Seth asked, genuine concern edging his normally mellow drawl.

"Maybe. She's pretty smart, and she's had all day to find a hole. You look up high, I'll try down low. She's got to be in the building somewhere."

Lisa was hunting through the bottom cupboards when Seth called out, "I found her."

"Oh, thank you!"

"I don't know about that," he said as she joined him by the couch. "She doesn't look too good."

That was an understatement.

Cleo, who loved to lounge on her window seat and admire the town below, had burrowed under a quilt and was curled up in a corner of the couch. Only the tip of her bushy brown tail was showing, which was why they'd missed her when they walked in.

Moving slowly, Lisa peeled back the quilt for a better look. Maine coons were one of the largest cats in existence, but Cleo had coiled herself up until she was the size of a large kitten. Without lifting her head, she blinked up at Lisa and opened her mouth in a silent plea for help.

When Lisa scooped her up, she went completely limp, and her head hung over Lisa's arm as if she didn't have the strength to hold it up. "Oh, baby, what's wrong?"

That got her another silent meow, and her heart seized with dread. Cleo was only two years old and had gotten a clean bill of health from the vet just before Thanksgiving. What could be so wrong?

Seth brushed a fingertip over Cleo's forehead, and she closed her eyes with a half-hearted whimper. "Has she been sick?"

"She's been kind of lazy the last few days, but she always gets like that in the winter. She didn't have much for lunch yesterday or the day before, but I figured it was because they were regular cat-food days." When he gave her a quizzical look, she explained, "She loves people food, but it's not good for her to have it all the time. So two days out of three she gets dry cat food, which she eats but isn't all that crazy about."

"How 'bout water?"

"I give her fresh every morning, but I don't measure it or anything. I don't know if she's been drinking it or not."

"Litter box?"

"What are you?" she demanded. "A vet?"

Considering the fact that she'd just taken his head off for asking a perfectly reasonable question, he took it in stride. "Just going down the list."

"You're right. I'm sorry." Rocking the cat in her arms, Lisa rubbed cheeks with her. "All right, my little Egyptian queen. I'm taking you to the vet."

"I can go with you. If you want," he added quickly, as if he was afraid he'd insulted her.

Lisa usually resented any implication that she couldn't handle something on her own, but this was different. If there was something seriously wrong with her beloved Cleo, she knew she'd lose it if she was alone.

"Thanks. That would be nice."

"My truck's still in the shop. How far away is the vet's office?"

"Just outside town, so we'll take my car. I'll give you directions."

After handing him her keys, she wrapped Cleo in the quilt to keep her warm. With the cat's long, thick fur, it was hardly necessary, but it made Lisa feel like she'd done something positive to help make her baby feel better.

Bless his heart, Seth didn't hesitate, just opened the door and locked it behind them. He didn't complain or even sigh while he wedged himself into her tiny car to make the short drive to the vet. No doubt about it, she mused with heartfelt gratitude. He was great to have around during an emergency.

Fortunately, Dr. Farnum was able to examine Cleo right away. She didn't react while he poked and prodded, not even when he drew blood and shoved a thermometer into a very uncomfortable place to take her temperature.

Checking the results, he frowned. "Well, she's running a fever, so we can assume she's got some kind of infection. The lab I use in Kenwood can tell us what kind, but not until tomorrow morning. With infections, twenty-four hours can make a big difference, so I think starting her on antibiotics is a good idea."

"Is it serious?" Lisa asked, stroking Cleo's fur as much to calm herself as the cat.

"I'm not sure at this point. We'll run a few more tests to find out for sure."

Despite his calm tone, Lisa's heart seized with fear. Because Cleo was so young, they'd never dealt with anything beyond shots and the occasional flea treatment. Glancing over at her listless cat, Lisa barely held back tears. Cleo was counting on Lisa to take care of her, but what would she do if the tests turned up something that couldn't be treated?

Dr. Farnum was watching her expectantly, and she knew he was waiting for her to approve the tests. She had to say something.

Hoping to sound more or less rational, she swallowed before answering. "Okay."

The door opened, and they were joined by a young woman dressed in puppy-and-kitten scrubs. Her name tag read "Brenda," and she honed in on Seth, flashing him an appreciative smile. Lisa must have been more upset than she thought, because she was seriously tempted to strangle the perky assistant for flirting with him instead of focusing on her very sick cat.

"Cleo shouldn't be left alone," the vet continued. "We don't want her getting dehydrated, so we need to monitor how much she's drinking. If you want, you can leave her overnight and we'll keep an eye on her for you."

"No." Lisa shook her head firmly. "She'll be more comfortable at home on the couch. Just tell me what to do, and I'll make sure it gets done."

The vet gave her an understanding smile. "I'll write out some instructions for you, then. Right now, we'll start those tests so you can get out of here."

Very gently, he lifted Cleo and handed her to Brenda.

"Hi, Cleo," she murmured, cuddling her much the way Lisa did. "Don't you worry about a thing, precious. We'll have you feeling like your old self in no time."

Brenda left the examining room, babbling a streak of soothing nonsense. Just before the door swung shut, Cleo looked back at Lisa and closed her big, golden eyes.

Tears stung Lisa's eyes, and she lowered her head in a heartfelt prayer. *Please, God. Don't take her away from me.*

"It'll be a little while," Dr. Farnum said in a patient tone that spoke of plenty of practice. "You can wait out in the lobby, or even go get something to eat if you want."

"No." More certain than she'd ever been in her life, Lisa met his gaze with a determined one of her own. It had been torturous to hand Cleo over to someone else as it was. She wasn't about to compound that by trotting off to get a snack as if nothing was wrong. "I'm not leaving here without Cleo."

When she felt a hand on her shoulder, she looked over at Seth. When she'd first met him, she'd read his features as cold and hard. The sympathy she saw in them now proved just how wrong she'd been about him.

"We'll wait out front, then. Thanks, Doc." *We.*

As Lisa numbly followed him through the

door, the word echoed in her head. While her family offered her a very large, loving safety net, she didn't often take advantage of it. What would it be like, she wondered, to have someone in your life who was always there beside you, willing to take on whatever life threw your way?

She and Seth settled on the bench nearest the exam rooms, and he gave her a smile of encouragement. Without saying a word, he took her hand for a gentle squeeze, holding it loosely while he looked around at posters of various animals from ferrets to thoroughbreds.

This was what Matt and Marianne had, Lisa realized with sudden clarity. Why they'd given up their independence to marry Caty and Ridge. They shared more than their houses, the family farm and the bills. They celebrated blessings that came along, like the new babies, and supported each other through the tough times. Blending together their individual hopes and dreams the way Lisa mixed paints on her palette until she found just the right color. They'd taken vastly different lives and melded them into something new, something that would go on forever.

She wanted that, too.

The strength of that emotion nearly knocked her off the bench, and Lisa clamped her mouth shut to keep the insane notion to herself. She was worried about Cleo, she reasoned, and Seth had been so sweet. It was only natural for her to reach out to someone who'd treated her so kindly. This man didn't mean anything more to her than any of the others she'd dated, her mind insisted stubbornly. When he was gone, her life would go on just as it had before she met him.

If only she could convince her heart of that, Lisa thought with a sigh, everything would be fine.

On the drive back to Lisa's place, Seth racked his brain for some encouraging words. The results of Cleo's most serious tests wouldn't be available until morning, and he'd seen enough fear to know Lisa was terrified of the possible outcome.

To his credit, the vet hadn't listed which diseases they were testing for but let his infection diagnosis stand for now. There was really no point in saying anything else. If it was something serious, chances were there was nothing anyone could do but put the suffering cat out of her misery.

What about Lisa's misery? Seth wondered as he parked the car and got out to open the passenger door. She loved her cat the way other people loved their children, and he hated to think how devastated she'd be if she had to make such a heart-wrenching decision.

Falling back on years of no-nonsense training, he concentrated on things he could control and tabled the rest. He went up the stairs and unlocked the front door, stepping aside to let Lisa go ahead of him with Cleo. When he snapped on the switch, the lit garlands twinkled down at him.

"Have those lights always blinked?" he asked.

Lisa stared at him as if he'd gone completely off his rocker. "They're not blinking."

Sure enough, when he looked again he saw she was right. Bizarre as it seemed, he had a sudden sensation of reassurance, as if someone had noticed Lisa was hurting and was trying to tell her everything would turn out okay.

Working too hard, Seth decided, flopping onto the couch and rubbing his hands over his face. He was imagining things.

"Could you watch Cleo while I get her some water?" Lisa asked.

That she trusted him with the ailing cat touched him deeply. She was relying on him, and for the first time it didn't make him want to turn tail and run.

"Sure. Come here, your highness." Taking her from Lisa, he carefully set her on the sofa. "Let's see what's going on in the world."

He clicked the TV on, flipping through channels until he found a show about crazy Christmas lights. It was fluff, but he thought the out-of-control Christmas decorations might cheer Lisa up a little. To his surprise, he felt the cushion shift as Cleo struggled to get up. She inched her way over, then struggled to climb into his lap.

Feeling honored and more than a little choked up, he spread the quilt on his lap and made a nest for her to settle into. With a contented feline sigh, she curled up, wrapped her tail around her nose and watched the TV through half-open eyes.

Coming in with a measuring cup of water and a yogurt container, Lisa pulled up short. "Did she do that?" she asked.

"Mostly. When I saw what she wanted, I helped her up." Suddenly, he wasn't sure he should have done it. "Is that okay?"

"Of course it is. I just can't believe it, is all." Shaking her head, she sat down beside him. "She really likes you."

Seth stroked her normally luxurious fur, which felt dry and stiff. "Once you get used to me, I'm not so bad."

"Very true," Lisa agreed with a shadow

of her usual smile. "Come on, baby. You need to get something in your stomach."

Cleo merely sniffed at the water and wouldn't touch the yogurt. After a couple of failed attempts, Lisa frowned. "She loves this flavor. Most days, she'd have inhaled it by now."

"I'm no cat expert, but let's try something."

Shrugging, Lisa handed over the snack Cleo was snubbing. Dipping his little finger into the yogurt, he touched it to the cat's nose. She completely ignored the spoon, but the blob on her nose must have bothered her because she licked it off. When he did it again, she gave him a semi-interested sideways glance.

One dollop at a time, he managed to feed her a tiny amount of yogurt. When he dipped some water into the spoon, she lifted her head just enough for a couple sips. Clearly exhausted by the effort, she dropped her head onto Seth's thigh and closed her eyes.

"That's amazing," Lisa said. "She hasn't eaten that much in three days."

"The antibiotic's probably kicking in, so she's feeling a little better."

"No, Seth," she corrected him with a grateful smile. "It's you. You're making her feel better. You're making *me* feel better, too."

He couldn't help grinning back. "At least I'm good for something."

"Lots of things, actually." Ducking under his arm, she cuddled in and stroked the now-dozing cat's long fur. "You're a handy guy to have around."

Since she'd made the first move, Seth figured it was okay to put his arm around her. Sitting there, snuggling on the sofa, watching TV, was incredible. Like he was meant to be there with Lisa, sharing some of the worry she was feeling. After everything she'd done for him, it felt good to repay some of that kindness.

"I'm not sure what to do about tomorrow," she confided while they watched a guy attach the last of Santa's reindeer to the roof of his house. "Cleo needs company, but I work from six to two."

"I'm sure if you explain things to Aunt Ruth, she'll give you some time off."

"Ordinarily she would," Lisa agreed. "But three of our waitresses have the flu, and we're really shorthanded. We've been so busy lately, I'd hate to call in at the last minute like this."

"Could someone at the farm watch Cleo for you?"

Lisa shook her head. "Everyone's in and out all day, but the house is empty most of the time. I want someone with her in case she needs something. I guess I'll just take her to the vet and let them watch her."

Her unhappy tone made it plain the animal clinic wasn't her favorite option. Careful not to disturb the sleeping cat, Seth slipped off his boots and crossed his feet on the coffee table. "Well, my schedule's pretty flexible. I could hang out here till you're done at the diner, then head over to the church. There's plenty of folks on the crew who know what they're doing, and if anybody needs me, they can call my cell."

Pulling her head away, she looked up at him with a hopeful expression. It was obvious she didn't want to impose on him, but he didn't see it that way. She needed help, and he could give it to her, simple as that.

"Are you sure?" she asked. "That's such a pain."

"Not really. Maybe I'll follow Cleo's example and get caught up on my sleep."

Bathing him in the most beautiful smile he'd ever seen, Lisa leaned over and kissed his cheek. "Thanks, Seth. That would be great."

Before she could fully retreat, he caught her cheek in his hand and drew her in for a real kiss. He'd been hoping for a chance to do that since their staged show at the diner, and it was worth the wait. When he pulled away, her eyes sparkled with approval.

"No mistletoe this time," she teased.

Not sure if she viewed that as a good thing or a bad thing, he kept his response light. "Nope, just us."

"I liked it."

Relief flooded in, and he chuckled. "You sound surprised."

"I am. A little," she added quickly. "I mean, we're not much alike, are we?"

Keeping his arm around her because he liked how it felt, Seth leaned back to give her some space. "That just keeps things interesting."

"I'm still going to Europe," she pointed out while she surfed for something else to watch.

Seth's instincts told him it was significant that she wouldn't look at him when she said it. Warning bells went off in every corner of his brain, screaming that things between them were rapidly snowballing out of his control. Determined to keep a grip on his sanity, he searched for a way to stop the slide without hurting her feelings.

"And I'm still going home when the church is fixed," he reminded her as gently as he could. "I'm not looking for long-term any more than you are."

"Okay," she said, still staring at the TV. "That works for me."

Her optimism sounded forced to him, and he wondered if he'd read her wrong. It wouldn't be the first time he'd misunderstood a woman, after all, and it probably wouldn't be the last. In the short time he'd known her, Lisa had come to mean a lot to him, and he'd do anything in his power to keep from hurting her. He wanted their relationship—whatever it was—to be absolutely clear.

With that in mind, he asked, "So where does that leave us?"

Tipping her head back, she gave him a saucy grin. "Friendly but unattached."

Her quick answer told him this arrangement was truly what she wanted, and he grinned back. "Sounds good."

On the screen, an old-fashioned theatrical opening came on, and she gasped. "*White Christmas!* This is my favorite Christmas movie."

"Really? I've never seen it."

Her mouth dropped open, and her eyes

widened with shock. "You're kidding, right? It's a classic, right up there with *It's a Wonderful Life*."

Seth was beat, but it took him less than a second to decide he'd hang around to watch it with her. "What's it about?"

"These two soldiers meet during World War II." Pausing, she gave him a hesitant look. "That might not work for you."

While he appreciated her sensitivity to his military past, he grinned to ease her mind. "I wasn't even alive back then."

"I mean, it's about a war. Not the whole movie, but—"

"Why don't we just watch for a while? If it's too much for me, I'll let you know."

"Okay."

As they watched the opening credits, Seth was glad to be headed home soon. Cozied up with her on the sofa, he tried without success to ignore the scent of flowers that followed her everywhere. As if that weren't bad enough, she fit perfectly against his side, filling a place that had been vacant for a long, long time.

He'd done his best to keep his emotional distance from Lisa Sawyer, he grumbled to himself, but every day it was getting harder to do. Her sunny, generous nature was irresistible, and he could no longer deny that she was starting to get under his skin. If he stayed in Harland much longer, he might do something really stupid.

Like tell her he was falling in love with her.

When she swiveled to face him, her solemn expression brought him back to the present with an unpleasant jerk. *Uh-oh,* he thought. *Serious time.*

"Seth, can I ask you something that's absolutely none of my business?"

He couldn't move without waking Cleo, but he forced himself to meet Lisa's gaze directly. After the way she'd stood by him, he owed her that much. "Sure."

"You were more than just a soldier, right?"

"I can't talk about it."

"I know, and I won't pry, but I can't help

wondering how bad it was for you. Being in a foreign country during a war, I mean."

Sifting through the grim history he'd fought to put behind him, he searched for something he could share without scaring or depressing her too much. "It was tough, but I was there with some of the best people I've ever met. We helped each other through."

"Until you came home," she said quietly. "Then you were on your own, and you couldn't really talk to anybody about it."

"My parents helped."

"Family can only do so much, though, can't they? Eventually, you have to stand on your own two feet and make your life work."

Those gentle, compassionate words sliced through every defense he'd created, straight into his heart. She'd nailed the emotion he felt most keenly, the one that drove him to keep going, even when it was hard. Equal parts determination and fear, it was a baffling combination he'd struggled to comprehend. In that moment he knew that, despite their obvious differences, he and Lisa had one very important thing in common.

He gently ran his finger along her soft cheek. "You really do understand, don't you?"

"I think so. Not the details, maybe, but I can follow the gist of it. Being strong and independent, doing things your own way." Pausing, she gave him one of her amazing smiles. "*That* I get."

As she snuggled against him again, he wanted to tell her how much that meant to him. How much *she* meant to him. It took every ounce of restraint he had to keep those words to himself, but somehow he managed. It was safer that way.

Chapter Nine

It was still dark when something woke Lisa from the first real sleep she'd gotten all night.

Her foggy brain cleared just enough to register the soft knocking on her door. Cleo shifted a little as Lisa untucked herself from their cozy place on the sofa and slowly stood up. Her legs and back were stiff from being cramped in one position all night, and she felt about a hundred years old as she shuffled to the door.

"Seth?" she whispered to avoid waking her cat.

"Room service," he murmured back.

When she opened the door, she caught

a whiff of fresh cranberry muffins and Ruthy's high-octane coffee. "You're the absolute best. What time is it?"

"Five." Glancing over at the mess on the sofa, he looked back at her with a grin. "I figured you wouldn't get much sleep, and it might be nice to have someone bring you breakfast."

"Very nice," she agreed with a yawn. "Thank you."

"No prob." Setting the bag and cup carrier on the coffee table, he hunkered down to give Cleo a gentle stroke on the head. "How's our furry patient doing?"

"No change, really. I couldn't get her to eat anything but she drank some water a while ago. That's probably a good sign, right?"

As tired as she was, Lisa fully recognized she was leaning heavily on someone who had much bigger problems than she did. She wasn't thrilled about that, but she appreciated Seth's reassuring look.

"Very good. Why don't you get ready for

work? I'll see if I can convince her to try some yogurt."

"Good luck."

Lisa took her coffee, downing several bracing swallows on her way to the closet. She got out a clean uniform and headed for the bathroom. By the time she'd showered and dressed, the caffeine had started to kick in and she was feeling more or less human.

How she looked was another matter entirely. She solved that with some extra concealer and foundation, topped off with a blush called "Perky Pink." After trying out a smile in the mirror, she decided the cosmetic commercials were right. There was nothing you couldn't hide with the right makeup.

Wary of bothering Cleo, Lisa eased the bathroom door open and peeked out. The scene in her living room made her heart go all warm and squishy.

Seth was sitting cross-legged on the floor with a spoon in one hand and a jar of yogurt in the other. While she watched in amazement, he dipped up some yogurt and ate some, leaving a little on the spoon. When he offered it to Cleo, she licked up the remainder and blinked up at Seth as if she was asking for more.

"That's incredible," Lisa approved as she walked through. "What's your secret?"

He shrugged, which she'd learned was his way of deflecting praise he wasn't comfortable with. One of these days, she vowed silently, she'd get the man to take a compliment.

"I don't know," he replied. "Maybe it's 'cause I'm eating it first, and she feels like she's being sneaky."

"Whatever it is, it's working." Going into the kitchen, she took a pill bottle off the windowsill and handed it to Seth. "I gave her one at midnight, and she should have another one at noon. It's a gel cap, and she doesn't like it," Lisa warned. "But it's important. Make sure she doesn't spit it out."

"Will do." Smiling, he resettled Cleo on her quilt and joined Lisa near the sink. "Go to work and try not to worry. When the vet calls you, let me know what he said."

The thought of hearing bad news shredded her already fragile nerves, and Lisa felt tears welling in her eyes. Staring at the sleeping ball of fluff on the sofa, she whispered, "What if it's bad news?"

Before she even finished her question, Seth gathered her into his arms and rested his cheek in her hair. "Then we'll figure it out, one way or another."

Any other guy she'd known would have confidently told her the cat would be fine, whether he believed it or not. But Seth would never lie to her just to make her feel better, even if it was what she wanted to hear more than anything.

Burying her face in his soft flannel shirt, she let a few tears fall. "I'm scared, Seth. I want her to be okay."

"I know." Kissing the top of her head, he wrapped her up a little tighter. "But sometimes life throws stuff at us that we can't control. We just have to do the best we can."

This was a man who understood that bitter truth more clearly than most. He lived with it every day, struggling against the memories that obviously still haunted him. If anyone knew the value of taking life as it came, it was Seth.

Pulling her head free, Lisa gazed up at him. "All night, I just held her and prayed. Do you think God heard me?"

With a sad smile, he kissed her forehead. "I think if He listens to anybody, He'd listen to you."

Lisa took the comment as a hint that Seth might be edging back toward the faith he so desperately needed. "Maybe He brought you here to Harland for a reason."

"Aunt Ruth's rehab work brought me here."

"That's done now," Lisa pointed out.

The frown Seth had been wearing darkened into an outright scowl. "I got roped into helping with the church project. Another week or so, it'll be far enough along a monkey could manage the rest."

"And you'll go home."

"For Christmas. After that—"

He shrugged as if it didn't matter all that much. While Lisa was eager to explore the world outside her tiny hometown, she couldn't imagine not having a place to return to. A place where she belonged, full of people who loved her and would welcome her back with open arms from wherever she'd been.

In her heart, she knew Seth wanted the same thing. And she was just the one to make it happen.

"Come to church with me on Sunday," she blurted before she could talk herself out of interfering. When he started to protest, she cut him off. "I'll buy you breakfast afterward."

Narrowing his eyes, he gave her a suspicious look. "Bribery, huh? Isn't that against the rules?"

"Come on, Seth," she prodded. "You set up, then you put everything away afterward. You know most of the folks who will be there, and it won't kill you to sit for an hour and listen to Pastor Charles's sermon. He's really good."

After a few moments of silence, Seth shook his head. "It's really not for me, but I appreciate you asking. You'd best get going or you'll be late."

He'd been so wonderful with Cleo—and her—that Lisa decided not to push. Seth was a grown man, after all, and he'd made it clear once again that he didn't want her poking around in his life. If he wanted to stagger along without faith, that was his choice. She only wished he'd give God another chance. She suspected that whatever had pushed him away was buried in his mysterious past, and he'd get past it if he put his mind to it.

One step at a time, she reminded herself. He'd come so far already, he was bound to get there with or without her help. Eventually. Most of the men she knew preferred to do things the hard way. Why, she had no clue, but apparently that trait came embedded in their Y chromosome.

"Okay." She smiled to let him know she wasn't insulted. "There's not much in the fridge, but help yourself to whatever you find. If things don't get crazy at the diner, I'll see you a little after two."

"No need to hurry. The queen and I are just gonna take a little nap."

He stretched out on the sofa and lifted the cat onto his chest, draping her quilt over top of them. After a halfhearted murmur of protest, Cleo cracked one eye open. Seeing it was Seth who'd disturbed her, she went right back to sleep.

Truly amazing, Lisa thought as she locked the door behind her. You had to love a guy who was so good with animals. That thought stopped her dead in the middle of the landing.

Did she love Seth?

Honestly, she wasn't sure. Getting to the point where she liked him had been challenging enough. Would loving him be twice as difficult? Her heart said no, but her mind had a different opinion altogether.

She was aware she was treading in very dangerous territory, and she forced herself back to reality. As she went down the steps, she reminded herself that she and Seth had agreed to the let's-be-friends approach. They enjoyed spending time together, but his plans didn't include her any more than hers included him. Whatever might be happening between them would end when he left Harland.

Maybe, that little voice in her head piped up. *Maybe not.*

She was really starting to hate that voice, she thought as she went through the diner's side entrance. It was annoying.

Fortunately, there was enough for her to do that she didn't have time to ponder anything beyond catering to their breakfast crowd. Mornings were always busy, and with only a few shopping days left until Christmas, folks were in full-on holiday mode. Some had started their vacations early, and relaxed laughter filled the dining room. As an added bonus, her tips were bigger than usual.

Today she'd probably make enough to pay for that guided tour of Montmartre, she thought with a smile of anticipation. The Sacred Heart Basilica there was impressive enough, but for Lisa the beautiful neighborhood held a more personal appeal. She'd actually be walking along the same streets as Monet and Picasso, spending time in the historic shops and cafés where they'd hung out during their lifetimes. How cool was that?

While she worked her way through the dining room, a lot of the talk was about how quickly the church project was coming along. She heard that the roof repairs would be complete on Monday, so their Christmas Eve service was a go. She was refilling Gus's mug with extra-strong coffee when her phone began singing Charlie Brown's "Christmas Time is Here."

The caller ID told her it was the vet's office, and she slipped into the storeroom for some privacy. If he was calling with bad news, she didn't want to fall apart in front of all these people.

"Good morning, Dr. Farnum. Do you have good news for me?"

"The best. I just heard from the lab, and all those scary tests came up negative. Cleo has a simple infection, and the antibiotic she's on should clear that up in another day or two."

"Oh, thank you!" Exhausted and relieved, Lisa sagged up against the wall to keep from falling down. "That's the best Christmas present I could've gotten."

"I know how you feel. I've gotten pretty fond of that spoiled cat of yours."

"Me, too. Thanks again."

They traded goodbyes and Lisa turned off her phone. Resting it against her forehead, she whispered a quick prayer of gratitude. She knew God had a lot of things to worry about, and it was comforting to know He'd heard her plea to leave Cleo with her awhile longer.

Once she'd composed herself, she called Seth. Before the first ring was done, she heard his groggy voice. "What'd the vet say?"

"She's fine," Lisa all but sang, too giddy to feel tired anymore. "The medicine she's on should fix her up in a couple days."

"That's great news. We couldn't have asked for better."

Even over the phone, he sounded as happy as she did. If he'd been there, she would have kissed him no matter who was watching.

"I'm so jazzed, I don't know what to do. Actually, yes, I do," she added impulsively. "When you're finished at the church, come by my place for supper. We'll celebrate."

"I thought you said you didn't cook."

His suspicious tone made her laugh. After the long night she'd had, it felt wonderful to be so upbeat. "I can toss together spaghetti and salad like nobody else. What do you say?"

"You don't mix 'em in the same bowl, do you?"

Picturing the mischievous glint in his eyes made her giggle. "Only if that's how you like them."

He chuckled. "Separate is fine. I'll see you later, then."

"I'm sure Cleo will be okay on her own, Seth. You can go if you want."

"Her highness is sound asleep on my chest. If I move her, she might have me beheaded or something."

If her cat was the real Cleopatra, he'd probably be right. "Good point. I guess I'll see you at two."

"I'll be here."

After they'd hung up, his parting words bounced around in her mind. Knowing he'd be at her place when she got off work improved Lisa's already stellar mood. Hard as she'd tried to keep her emotional distance from the lanky carpenter, somewhere along the line she'd gotten attached to him.

Time and again, he'd proven himself both reliable and fun to be around. All along, she'd known he wouldn't be in town forever, but for the first time Lisa faced the stark truth. Seth wasn't like the other guys who'd strolled into and out of her life. She was really going to miss him when he left.

Because she hated to ruin a perfectly wonderful morning brooding about something she couldn't change, she put it out of her mind and got back to work.

* * *

Just after two, Seth handed a much perkier Cleo back to her grateful owner and headed over to the church. Following the schedule he'd designed, shifts of volunteers came in throughout the day, checking tasks off Seth's list as they were completed. They had a week left, and only two big jobs remained: finishing the newly framed wall and replacing the heavy-duty blue tarp with a proper section of roof.

The wall wouldn't be much of a problem, he judged. Their siding contractor had matched the old clapboards perfectly, and his crew was outside nailing them on with professional efficiency. Two sisters who ran a painting company had donated material and their crew's labor to paint the outside of the entire church a crisp white that made the old color look more like gray. They were already on-site, ready to start as soon as the siding was complete.

In short, everything was on track and just slightly over budget. When Seth mentioned the latter to Pastor Charles, the man had just winked and assured him that was no problem. Apparently, more money had appeared out of thin air. Seth suspected at least some of it was coming from his aunt, which only made him prouder to be part of this project that was so important to her. The chapel might not be completely finished by Christmas Eve, but folks would be warm and dry and have places to sit.

Satisfied with the new wall, he turned his attention to the roof. It was a sunny day, so they'd pulled the blue tarp away to allow the light in. Looking up at the square hole, he judged it would take a couple of hours to lay the plywood and reshingle the quarter-section of roof. Or, he thought with a grin, they could pull off decades' worth of patches and do it right.

Inspired by the idea, he grabbed a roofer's harness and pulled himself up the studded wall for a better look. He tied himself to one of the beams, yanking the strap to make sure the clasp was secure. Walking across the intact section, he felt soft spots here and there where water had worked its way in and started rotting the old boards. Taking the chisel from his tool belt, he lifted several corners and found that many of the shingles were damp on the bottom.

A spot-check showed him pretty much the same over the whole roof. The next soaking rain would probably end up leaking into the sanctuary, ruining all the interior work they'd put in. He hated wasting time and energy, and he had no doubt the members of the congregation would feel the same. But a whole new roof would be expensive. While everyone might agree the work needed to be done, where would they find the money to pay for it?

"What're you doing up there? Trying to break your neck?"

Hearing Jim Canfield's very familiar bark, Seth looked down at him through the new roof supports.

"I'm tied off." To prove it, he rattled the clasp on his harness.

Glowering darkly, Jim crossed his arms in an angry gesture. "That don't answer my first question."

"Actually, I'm wondering if it might make sense to replace the whole roof." Settling on one knee, Seth glanced at the intact section, then back down at their self-appointed roofing expert. "I'm not sure how long it'd take, but I was hoping you and I could talk it over."

Something like respect softened the older man's weathered scowl, and he made some kind of thinking noise. "Roofs are expensive, y'know."

"Actually, I have no idea," Seth hedged in an effort to make his adversary feel as though he had the upper hand. It was a trick he'd learned years ago from his martial-arts trainer, and he was hoping it would work for him now. "Maybe you could educate me on that."

After a few moments, Jim muttered something not entirely unflattering. "Come down here, boy. I'm getting a crick in my neck."

Taking that for the crusty man's version of approval, Seth quickly descended to join him inside. He was surprised when Jim shook his head with a grin.

"You really want to do a good job on this, don't you?" he asked, sounding more than a little surprised.

"Yes, sir. What happened here was just short of a tragedy, and I want to make it right."

"So do I." After a long pause, Jim rubbed a hand over the back of his neck. "I suppose I should've said that before, instead of just being bullheaded and blocking you all the time."

"This is your church, so the job's personal for you," Seth replied easily. "I understood."

"I appreciate that." Clearing his throat, he added, "Most folks don't get that about me."

"I do. I'm the same way."

"My wife told me I was handling it badly, taking everything the wrong way. I really just wanted to be in on the planning, y'know? I guess it burned me when Pastor Charles put you in charge."

They stood there for an awkward moment, and Seth recognized that it had taken a lot of courage for this man to open up to him. Because of that, he decided to give Jim what he'd wanted from the start. "Totally understandable. I could really use your expertise now, though. I can see the roof's shot, but I have no idea how to fix it properly."

Offering his hand, he smiled to show there were no hard feelings on his end. Their quick handshake erased the tension that had crackled between them since their first awkward meeting, and Jim actually managed a creaky smile.

"All right, then," he said with an unexpected twinkle in his dark eyes. "Let's go on up and see what needs doing."

Seth gave him the harness and motioned for him to go up first. While he waited, he felt his eyes slide toward the boxed-in stained-glass window. He was still a little shaky on the faith thing, but he couldn't help wondering if Jim Canfield's turnaround was some kind of a sign.

* * *

"So," Seth finished his story while he set Lisa's table, "nobody needs to worry about getting dripped on during your Christmas Eve service."

More than a little impressed, Lisa shook her head as she dumped spaghetti into a colander to rinse it out. "Jim's the most stubborn, cantankerous man in town. How on earth did you get on his good side?"

"I'm not sure," Seth confided as he took the salad bowl from the counter. "I guess when he realized I was in it for the right reason, he changed his mind about me."

Laughing, she put on the snowman-shaped oven mitts her nephew and niece had given her last year and pulled the garlic bread from the oven. "He must have caught the Christmas spirit or something."

"Yeah," he said softly, "I was thinking the same thing."

Completely stunned, she stood there with the tray in her hands and just stared at him. For the first time in a while, he looked the way he had the first time she'd met him.

Uncomfortably shy, to the point that her heart went out to him.

Setting the bread down on the stove, she turned to him with an encouraging smile. "That's good, Seth."

"You think?"

"Very good," she added, nodding enthusiastically. "If you're starting to think that way after what you've been through, that's amazing."

"I didn't get there on my own." Looking down at the salad, he added, "It's mostly because of you."

Flattered beyond belief, she took a step closer. "Me?"

"Yeah," he said, lifting his eyes to meet hers. "I had it once, you know, just like you. I lost it somewhere along the way, and I wasn't sure how to get it back so I quit trying."

"That's totally understandable." Deciding to take a huge risk, she added, "God understands, too. He's just been waiting for you to find your way back."

"Maybe."

"Definitely."

Shaking his head with uncertainty, Seth moved down the counter to take the salad spoon from her tool crock. It was obvious he wasn't comfortable confiding these very personal feelings in her, and Lisa felt as if they'd gone several steps back in their friendship. Once again, she was reaching out to him while he retreated from her.

This time she wasn't letting him get by with it.

Her kitchen was so tiny, there were only a few steps between them. She covered them quickly, then reached up to frame his perfectly sculpted face in her hands. Something like hope kindled in his eyes, and she smiled as she brought his mouth to hers.

In a single heartbeat, she was circled in his arms. The strength that coursed through him flowed around her in a current that actually took her breath away. When she eased back, the emotion showing on his face mirrored her own feelings.

He flashed her a very male grin. "What'd I do to deserve that?"

Say it, that tiny voice whispered. *Tell him you love him.*

"It's for being so great with Cleo," she sputtered. "I really appreciate all your help."

"I mixed the salad, too," he teased, drawing her back in for another kiss.

Even though she knew it was a mistake, she went along. Here in her cozy studio, with a warm supper and an even warmer companion, she had the sensation of being encased in a cocoon. It was her favorite time of year, Cleo was fine and Seth was here.

Next week, he'd be gone, and she knew she'd miss him terribly. But here and now, wrapped up in his arms, was the only thing she wanted to think about.

Chapter Ten

Sunday afternoon, Lisa met Seth at the work shed in Gus's backyard. The new benches were ready, and now they were going to finish all twenty of them with the stain she'd mixed and brought with her. Hopefully, they'd be done before midnight.

"It's pretty chilly today," Seth commented as he slid open the door and carried the boxful of cans inside. "I started the heater up earlier, so I hope you're okay."

"I'm a country girl," Lisa assured him. "I'm tougher than I look."

He snapped on the lights, and she stood there for a minute taking it all in. Gus's style to the core, the workshop was decorated in early male, complete with mounted deer heads and a rainbow trout the size of a small shark. How he'd reeled it in was beyond her. In the corner, an ancient potbelly stove was cranking out enough warmth to make it comfortable, and she took off her jacket while Seth closed the door.

When she saw what he'd been working on, she gasped in surprise. "Seth, they're beautiful!"

The church had had the exact same pews since the day the original builders put them in. The tree disaster had wiped out half of them, leaving the others intact. That meant they had to either replace them all, which was simpler but more expensive, or create new ones that matched the old.

Based on finances and sentiment, the congregation had voted for the second option. Seth had done a masterful job, Lisa thought as she examined them up close. Except for the raw oak, she would never have been able to tell them apart. From the rounded edges to the flowers carved into the aisle panels, they were exactly the same.

Completely amazed, she turned to stare at him. "You had to make ten of these. How on earth did you get them done with everything else you've got going on?"

"No TV."

For a second, she thought he was serious, which was depressing. How could someone living in this century not have a TV? Then he added one of his rare grins, and she laughed. "You had me going there for a second."

"That was the idea."

"You sound like Matt. I can never tell when he's kidding, either."

Opening the stove door with a poker, he tossed in a couple of small logs. "You make that sound like a good thing."

"Oh, it is. He drives me nuts, but I love him to pieces." Concerned that Seth might think she meant she loved him, too, Lisa quickly added, "If we're going to be sitting on these Christmas Eve, I'd better get started."

"Sounds good." Reaching up to a high

shelf, he turned on the old radio and asked, "What kind of music do you like?"

She blinked at him as if he'd lost his mind. "Christmas."

"Right. What was I thinking?"

The lightness in his tone made her smile. She'd heard it more lately as he became more comfortable with her and opened up a crack at a time. Because she was female, she couldn't deny that she was drawn to this handsome, complex man. He was nothing like the guys she normally dated, but that was part of his unique charm. Now that they had some time alone together, she wondered if his feelings for her had moved beyond the let's-be-friends stage to something more.

Deciding it was time to force the issue out in the open, she kept her eyes on her moving paintbrush. "Seth, do you like me?"

"Sure." She glanced over, and he grinned. "A lot."

"And I like you."

"That's good to hear."

Wiping a cloth over the wet stain to set

it, she went for broke. "So do you think we should do anything about it?"

After a few moments, he sighed and set down the brush he'd been using. Crossing the floor, he slipped his arms around her and gazed down at her with an expression somewhere between a smile and a frown.

"Lisa, I think you're amazing. Probably the most amazing woman I've ever met. You're pretty and funny, and you make me feel like Superman. But I've still got a few pieces missing. Big pieces. Until I find them, I'm not ready for anybody. Especially not you," he added, dropping a kiss on her forehead.

She was completely lost. "What do you mean especially not me?"

"You deserve a man who can give you everything he's got, share everything he is with you."

"And you can't ever do that," she finished, picking up what he didn't say from the misery clouding his eyes. "I could learn to live with that."

Scowling, he shook his head with finality. "You shouldn't have to."

But I want to almost popped out before her brain kicked in and stopped her. Seth was worth the compromise, her heart was certain of it. The trouble was, she knew herself well enough to realize it would always bother her, that part of him that existed in the shadows just beyond her reach.

"Seth, will you please tell me what happened? I don't need top secret details, just the basics. I'm not being nosy, and I promise not to tell anyone. I just think it would really help you to get it out."

After a long pause, he finally answered the questions that had plagued her since she first met him.

"It was the kind of mission you don't hear about in the news. Twelve of us went in." He swallowed hard. "Two of us came out."

As the silence stretched on, she feared he'd gotten stalled in his horrific past. Gently, she nudged him forward. "Is that when you hurt your shoulder?"

"Yeah. Fortunately, my buddy was a medic.

He packed it to keep me from bleeding to death while we hiked to our extraction point. The chopper came in, and we ran for it." Stopping again, he heaved a deep, bone-weary sigh. "He shoved me inside, but a sniper got him in the back before he could pull himself up. When we landed at our base, I was the only one of my unit left."

Lisa's heart ached for those brave young men, but especially for the one standing in front of her, still in such horrendous pain. It took everything she had not to break down in tears. "I'm glad you escaped, but it must have been horrible for you. I'm so sorry."

"It's tough being the only survivor. At least that's what the shrink told me. I knew he was trying to help me, but it never really worked. I still don't know why," he confided in a miserable voice.

"You need time," Lisa said, resting her hand on his cheek in a comforting gesture. "When we lost my dad, it felt like we'd never be able to get past it. Somehow, we each figured out a way to remember him but go on with our lives. One day, when you're ready, you'll do the same."

Seth pulled away from her slowly, as if it hurt him to do it. "We should get back to work."

How many people had he retreated from this way? she wondered as she resumed her staining. While she now understood his reasons, she couldn't help thinking there was a way around them. She was an out-side-the-box kind of girl, accustomed to creating art out of nothing but an idea and a bunch of colors. Maybe she could come up with a solution.

In the meantime, she needed to concentrate on what she was doing. Blending various shades of brown to just the right shade of walnut wasn't easy, but she kept at it until she found the perfect match for the decades' worth of color on the old pews. As she brushed it on and wiped some of it off, she felt tremendous satisfaction watching Seth's raw carpentry become a finished product.

She was more than a little proud of her

contribution, she had to admit. Even though it was one of the most difficult tasks she'd ever attempted, the results were proving to be worth the effort.

"How's this?" she asked.

He came over for a closer look, walking around the bench to see it from different angles. "Beautiful." Grinning at her, he added, "You made it perfect, Lisa. Just like I knew you would."

She thought she heard a little extra emotion humming under the surface of his praise, but she quickly put the idea out of her head. Seth had made it clear how he felt about her, and why he felt that way. Because she valued everyone's right to their opinion, she'd never tried to change any guy's mind about her, one way or the other. She wasn't about to start now.

With the melancholy "Merry Christmas, Darling" playing on the radio, Lisa squared her shoulders and sifted through the facts Seth had laid in front of her. She needed wide-open honesty, and his past would always be closed to her. If their relationship was ever going to move past the let's-be-friends stage they were in now, she'd have to accept that limitation and love him in spite of it.

Could she live with that? And more importantly, did she want to?

Lisa was manning the lunch counter Tuesday morning when John sauntered through the door and plopped onto a stool.

"Hey," he said with a yawn.

"Hey, yourself," she replied, laughing. "What are you doing here? I thought you and Matt were helping to finish the interior walls at the church today."

"We were, but there's six of us and we kept getting in each other's way, so Seth sent me over for coffee."

It didn't take a genius to figure out why John had been elected gopher. "Did you break one of those nice new windows?"

"Course not. I'm not an idiot."

He didn't volunteer any more information, but she wasn't letting him off that easy. Born troublemaker that he was, there were still only so many problems he could cause this early in the morning. "Who did you hit with a hammer?"

"Nobody." When she tilted her head in disbelief, he muttered, "Okay, I *almost* hit somebody."

Laughing, she filled in the extremely obvious blank. "Matt."

"How do you know these things?" he demanded with a scowl. "It's spooky."

"Ordinarily, I'd say feminine intuition," she replied breezily. "With you, it's just logic. Seth didn't want Matt to kill you."

John chuckled. "Yeah, he was pretty mad. I almost forgot—he wanted me to tell you the parts are in for your transmission. If you bring your car out to the farm, he'll get it fixed up for you."

"Fabulous! That clunking noise keeps getting louder and louder." Flipping back to waitress mode, she asked, "How much coffee do you need?"

"I dunno. For the crew, I guess." Mild panic crossed his face, and he made a good show of patting the pockets of his jeans. He might have convinced a stranger, but Lisa knew it was all an act. "It's free, right? I don't have my wallet."

"Would it matter if you did?"

Grinning at the dig, he shook his head. "Empty as usual."

"Big surprise," she scolded with a sigh. He was three years older than she was, but with his knack for losing and forgetting things, sometimes he acted a lot more like the youngest than she did. "How many folks have you got over there today?"

Looking up as if that would help him find the answer, he took a few seconds before answering. "Ten. I think."

"I'll do twelve, just to be sure."

"Sounds good."

As she pulled out three carriers and lined up a dozen to-go cups, he swiveled his stool back like a big, fidgety kid. "You look worried. What's up?"

She did? Until then, Lisa was confident she had her emotions under control. While John wasn't her first choice as a confidant, she decided to give it a try. "Just thinking about someone."

"Seth?" When she nodded, he asked, "What about him?"

While she poured coffee, she answered, "I want to get him a Christmas present, but I have no idea what to buy. What's your favorite thing to get from a girl?"

"You mean, besides her phone number?"

Lisa glared at him, and he laughed shamelessly. She should have known better than to ask her hound of a brother for advice on guys. "Forget it. I'll figure it out on my own."

"Why don't you ask Ruthy? She probably knows what he's into."

"Her granddaughter is playing Clara in *The Nutcracker* in Charlotte, so she went there for the show. She won't be back until tomorrow night, and he's leaving soon, so I need to get him something today."

"Because?"

"Because I want to, you doof." After fastening the top on the last cup, she scowled at him the way Marianne did when he was being impossible. Which was frequently. "Are you going to help me or not?"

"Call his mom. She'll know." Stacking the coffee trays, he grinned at her on his way out the door.

"Thanks."

While she set fresh pots of coffee brewing, Lisa seriously considered John's suggestion. It proved how desperate she was that she didn't reject it right off the bat. Finally, she admitted it was a horrible idea. She didn't have the Hansens' phone number and even if she did, what would she say?

Hi, this is Lisa Sawyer. You don't know me, but I'm trying to buy a present for your son. Do you happen to know what he'd prefer?

If the woman didn't hang up on her immediately, Lisa would be amazed. But while she was spraying disinfectant on the counter and wiping it down, a slightly more rational approach popped into her head. Seth's mother was Ruthy's sister, and Lisa was Ruthy's goddaughter. That meant they were almost related. It was worth a shot, anyway.

Going to the pass-through window, she called out, "Tammy, I'm going to take my break now, okay?"

"Sure, I can handle the dining room for a few. Hurry back, though."

"I'll be in Ruthy's office if you need me."

The cook nodded, and Lisa walked toward the office at the back of the building. Typical Ruthy, it was a charming mix of the old and the new. The antique cherry desk and cabinets looked as if they'd fit right in at a stately antebellum home, but the sleek laptop was the latest model.

Half closing the door behind her, Lisa settled into the chair and wiggled the mouse to wake up the computer. She would never snoop in someone's personal files, but she thought it was all right to search through the Fayetteville online white pages. There were several Hansens listed, but one jumped out at her.

William and Sarah. Knowing her godmother's solid Christian background, Lisa checked the other options but didn't find any Biblical names. Instinct told her the names Ruth and Sarah went together, so she took out her cell phone and dialed the number.

A woman answered, and Lisa reminded herself to stay calm so she wouldn't sound like a lunatic stalker. "Hello, this is Lisa Sawyer. May I speak with Sarah Hansen, please?"

"This is she."

"We haven't met, but I'm Ruth Benton's goddaughter." Lisa figured that was the best opening. If Sarah didn't know Ruth, she'd try the next name on the list.

To her relief, the woman said, "I thought 'Sawyer' sounded familiar. Your family lives in Harland, right?"

"Yes, ma'am." Knowing she didn't have much time, Lisa got right to the point. "I hate to bother you, but I was wondering if you could help me with something."

"I'm not sure how, but I'll try."

After Lisa explained why she was calling, Sarah laughed. "You're the one, aren't you?"

"Which one?"

"The girl who's made Seth sound happier than he has in ages. I keep asking who he's seeing, but he says he's been so busy he doesn't have time to date. I knew he was fudging."

"Actually, he's not," Lisa corrected her quickly. "We're just friends."

"You want to buy a gift for a man who's just a friend? Why?"

Because he's incredible, Lisa almost blurted out before she stopped herself. Instead, she chose something a little less gooey. "He's been tutoring me in some foreign languages for a trip I'm taking. He's put in a lot of time and been so patient, I'm trying to find a way to thank him."

"Saying it usually does the trick with him," his mother pointed out.

"I want to get him something special. A gift that would mean a lot to him personally."

"That's so sweet of you. He's not much for googaws, but let me think a minute."

Sarah was quiet for almost that long, and Lisa hoped she'd come up with a good idea before she had to get back to work.

"Well," Sarah finally said, "he used to have a pewter key chain with a charm that said 'be strong and courageous.' Bill's father gave it to Seth, and he carried it in memory of his grandfather after he passed away. Seth lost it just before he was hurt."

"It's from the Book of Joshua, right? When my brothers graduated from high school, my dad gave them each a watch with that verse engraved on the back."

"What a wonderful idea," Sarah approved. "It was Seth's favorite Bible quote when he was younger. Before—before things changed."

Lisa heard a tapping on the door and glanced up to find Tammy pointing toward the dining room, her mouth open in a silent scream.

"I have to go now, Mrs. Hansen. Thanks so much for your help."

"You're very welcome. And thank you for being such a good friend to Seth. If you're ever in Fayetteville, please stop by. I'd love to meet you in person."

"Next time you and your husband are here visiting Ruthy, come out to the farm. You're always welcome."

"How sweet of you. Merry Christmas, dear."

"Merry Christmas to you, too."

Switching off her phone, Lisa mentally braced herself for a rush and followed Tammy back into the diner.

"This is great," Marianne approved as she and Lisa strolled down Main Street. "I'm so glad you called me. I can't remember the last time we went shopping together, just the two of us."

"It's been way too long," Lisa replied as they stopped near a group of carolers dressed in Victorian costumes. Relatively on pitch, they really seemed to be enjoying their version of "Good King Wenceslas."

"They're like something out of a Dickens

book," Marianne whispered. "Only more cheerful."

Lisa smiled agreement, and when the singers were done, the crowd that was circled around them applauded. The women curtsied, the men tipped their tall hats and they continued down the sidewalk to spread their Christmas cheer.

"I love it here." Marianne sighed, looking around the festive downtown with a smile. "I don't like how it happened, but I'm so glad God brought the kids and me back from Chicago."

"Yeah, me too." Lisa gave her a quick hug around the shoulders. "I missed you when you were gone."

Marianne turned to her, suddenly serious. "I'm thrilled that you're going to Europe, because I know it's always been a dream for you. But I have to be honest. I'll be just as thrilled when you come home."

The unexpected revelation from her normally reserved sister brought tears to Lisa's eyes. Emotion clogged her throat, and she swallowed before speaking. "I'll feel the same way, Mare. I'm going to miss you, too."

After a long, adoring look, Marianne gave her a shaky smile. "At least I know you won't stay away too long. I'll have your cat."

Laughing, the two of them turned into Harland Jewelry, which the window proudly proclaimed had been in business since 1879. Several brightly lit cases sat at angles to one another, filled with watches and anything you could think of made from gold, silver and diamonds. Anniversary clocks, silver baby cups and crystal goblets lined the glass shelves on the walls, everything accented by holly garlands and tiny white lights.

"Wow," Lisa breathed. "It's all so beautiful, I don't know where to start."

"These chunky silver bracelets are gorgeous, really masculine."

"Seth works with his hands constantly. He'd have to take it off all the time so it wouldn't get caught in a saw or something."

Marianne stared at the display a little

longer, and Lisa grinned. She knew what Ridge was getting in his stocking this year.

"What are you looking for, then?" Marianne asked as she glanced around. When Lisa relayed what Seth's mother had told her, Marianne frowned. "Are you sure that's a good idea? He might not want to be reminded of how he lost it."

"His grandfather gave it to him when he was younger," Lisa argued. "It will make him think of a better time in his life."

"Maybe." After a few seconds, Marianne admitted, "You know Seth better than I do."

Not much, Lisa realized, but her intuition was usually bang on, and it was telling her to do this for Seth. "I just want him to have something to remember me by after he goes home."

That got Marianne's attention. Turning, she pinned Lisa with her suspicious-mom look. "Is there something you haven't told me about this guy?"

"Of course not," Lisa hedged. "I tell you everything."

"Since when?"

"I tell you the important stuff," Lisa corrected. "If it's really big, I tell the boys."

"Just be sure you keep that up, even if you end up living across the ocean somewhere. Okay?"

Smiling at her big sister, Lisa added a hug for good measure. "You got it."

Chapter Eleven

The rest of the week was a flurry of activity around Seth's various projects. He sealed the floors in Aunt Ruth's apartments, finished installing her new stainless-steel commercial dishwasher and bolted the pews onto the refurbished floor at the church. By the time everything was finished, he was whipped. He hadn't been this tired in so long, he'd forgotten what it felt like.

But it was a good tired, he told himself as he drove his good-as-new pickup over to Lisa's apartment the day before Christmas Eve. He'd accomplished a lot in the past month, and it had left him feeling stronger than he had in years.

"Decorating the tree's kind of a family tradition," he said as he helped Lisa crate up the portrait she'd been working on since before he first met her. "Are you sure I won't be intruding?"

"Not a bit," she assured him with a bright smile. "The more, the merrier. Besides, I can't carry this thing by myself."

"Now we've got the truth." He chuckled while they strapped the protective frame together. "I'm the muscle."

"Somebody has to be. I'm just for looks." Adopting a fish-faced supermodel pose, she laughed and he joined her.

Laughter came a lot easier to him these days, and he knew he had Lisa to thank for finding that in him again. He just didn't know how.

"You're sure you don't need a ride back into town?" he asked.

"Matt's been working on my car out at the farm today, and he said it's ready. Something about the transmission," she added with a sour face. "He's a mechanic, so he only charges me for the parts."

"Farmer and mechanic. Good combination."

"That depends on which day you ask him."

Seth laughed. "I'm sure it does."

Very carefully, he laid the framed canvas down flat in the bed of his pickup and cinched cargo straps over it to keep it from moving. They only had to go a few miles, but he was determined to get Lisa's precious family gift to the farm in the same condition it was in now.

He opened the passenger door for her, and she gave him one of her bright, beautiful smiles. "Thank you."

"No problem." He climbed in the other side and eased the truck out of its spot to avoid disturbing his cargo. Lisa was chattering like an excited blue jay and about a mile out, he said, "You're psyched about giving your family that portrait, aren't you?"

"Yeah. I've been working on it a long time, and I can't wait for them to see it."

Suddenly, she gasped. "Oh, no! I forgot to get heavy-duty hooks to hang it with."

"Don't worry." Seth patted the chest pocket of his denim jacket. "I brought some. Gus said you could use them to hang an elephant, so I think they'll do."

She blew out a sigh so deep, it ruffled her bangs. "I'm glad you thought of that. It would have been such a bummer not to be able to hang the portrait up right away."

"I'm curious why you're bringing it now. It seems like the kind of thing you'd do on Christmas Day."

Reaching over, she rubbed his shoulder. "You were so encouraging while I worked on it, I wanted you to be there when they see it for the first time. Plus, they all asked to see you again so they could say goodbye before you leave."

Glancing over, Seth asked, "How about you? Are you going to say goodbye, too?"

"Not tonight," she replied quickly. "Tonight is for enjoying. I'll say it tomorrow."

She turned to stare out the window, and Seth thought he heard a trace of regret in her voice. He was feeling some himself, and his heart leaped at the possibility that Lisa might miss him. He was tempted to tell her he could stay, at least until New Year's, but his characteristic reserve made him hold back.

Settling permanently in Harland wasn't in his plans, so extending his visit would only delay the inevitable. Since she was going to Europe in the spring, it was probably best for both of them if he left now.

Or was it?

Dense as he was about some things, Seth knew his own heart. It wanted him to stay with Lisa and see where their relationship would go. The trouble was, he had absolutely nothing to offer her, and she deserved to have everything in the world.

Besides, he was tired of roaming around the world, and she was just getting started. Then again, maybe traveling with Lisa wouldn't be so bad. No one would be shooting at him, after all, and he could just enjoy himself. With the money he had saved up, if he was sensible he could probably be gone for a year or more.

Just one problem, the voice of reason reminded him: she hadn't asked him to go along. All they'd done was share a few kisses, and she was eager to spread her wings and fly. The last thing she probably wanted right now was to be tangled up with a guy still learning how to walk.

Thankfully, his pointless mulling ended as he pulled in at the Sawyer farm. Easing his truck in beside the back porch, he opened Lisa's door and unhooked her painting. As they carried it up the steps, he could smell pork roast and something sweet to go along with it. Through the window he heard Kyle and Emily singing "Rudolph," with the extra phrases kids liked to throw in.

"Like a lightbulb!" they shouted as Lisa opened the door.

When they saw her, they ran over and almost knocked her down with a tag-team hug.

"Seth, Aunt Lisa, wait till you see the

tree!" Kyle exclaimed, motioning to the archway. "It's humongous!"

"I picked it out," Emily informed them in a very grown-up voice. "It's the prettiest one ever."

"Whoa." Looking through the archway into the living room, Seth approved her choice with a low whistle. The large space was dominated by a blue spruce whose top ended just a few inches short of the vaulted ceiling. "Nice job."

The little girl's blue eyes sparkled at the praise. "Thank you."

The kids raced away, and Marianne came around the island with a curious look at their package. "What's this?"

"Oh, just a little something for over the fireplace," Lisa replied casually, leading Seth toward the spot. "I thought it would make a nice holiday decoration."

Marianne gave Seth a questioning glance, but he was careful to keep his expression neutral. He didn't want to spoil Lisa's surprise by mistake. Near the fireplace, they met up with three guys drowning in a sea of ornament boxes and tangled Christmas lights.

"Here's some blue replacement bulbs." Taking them out of a box, Caty held them up from her seat in the rocking chair. "I'd bring them over, but I can't get up."

"Stay right there," Matt told her sternly. "We haven't done our Lamaze class yet, and I'm not crazy about winging an early delivery."

"Okay." Rocking a little, she smiled over at Seth and Lisa. "Happy tree day, you two."

"Lisa's got something for us," Marianne announced, motioning to the crate. "The lights can wait."

"Works for me," John agreed quickly, dropping his strand.

Laughing, Ridge strolled over to join everyone in front of the mantel. After some shifting around, they all fixed expectant looks on Lisa.

"I don't have a big speech or anything," she said. "I've been working on something for all of us, and I wanted to give it to you now."

Taking his cue, Seth undid the straps and helped her lift the portrait from its protective frame. Because John was standing off to the side, he saw it first.

"Lisa," he whispered, "that's incredible."

The others pressed in for a better view, and Seth moved away to give Lisa the spotlight. The painting had been a labor of love for her family, and she'd earned every compliment they could give her.

"It's amazing," Marianne said, gently touching the canvas. "It looks just like a photograph."

Lisa beamed with pleasure. "That's the idea. Our copies of that photo won't last forever, but this will."

"We shouldn't hang it here," Marianne protested. "The sunlight will fade the paint."

"No, it's fine," Lisa assured her. "I finished it with a sealant that will keep the paint from fading or cracking."

"Smart," Matt approved with a nod.

That single word from her cherished older brother made Lisa's chin tremble a little,

Seth noticed. Hoping to keep her from crying, he pulled the anchors from his pocket and stepped forward. "John, you want to give me a hand with these?"

They hammered in the hardware, then hung the painting in its place of honor. While he was buying the hangers, Seth had found two tiny battery-powered spotlights. He pulled them from another pocket and placed them on the mantel. Switching them on, he angled them so they lit the painting to its best effect.

The slight red tint of the mahogany frame perfectly complemented the summery colors in the portrait. The green grass, the light filtering down through the tree branches, the cheery plaid blanket the family was sitting on, everything blended into a heartwarming memory of the Sawyers' past. One that would be the same a hundred years from now as it was tonight.

Grinning at his sister, John put an arm around her shoulders. "It's great, Lisa. I can smell the fried chicken."

Her laugh was part joy and part relief,

and she hugged him around the waist as if she was still a little girl. Then she surprised Seth by reaching out her other arm to him. "I had a hard time with Mom's face until Seth helped me. Doesn't she look beautiful?"

Everyone rushed to compliment him, and he thanked them with a nod. This was Lisa's moment, and he didn't want to steal any of the credit from her. But it felt good to be recognized for something he'd done, instead of slinking away to avoid being seen.

Tonight, for the first time since coming home two years ago, he felt as though he truly belonged right where he was. It was a good feeling.

It was past nine when the kids hung the last two ornaments on the biggest tree the Sawyers had ever dragged in from their woodlot. Tired but happy, Lisa looked over at Seth, who'd pitched in as usual to help them decorate the higher branches. She was so glad he'd been with them tonight, sharing a festive meal and helping them trim the tree before heading back to his own family.

She would miss him, but she'd come to terms with his leaving. It was best for both of them, and she'd think of the multitalented carpenter fondly every time she ordered a meal in a European restaurant and ended up with what she wanted.

Marianne took the antique crystal star from its egg crate and held it up high. "Who wants to do the star?"

Both Kyle and Emily piped up, arguing it was their turn. Honestly, Lisa didn't know how they remembered from one year to the next, but one of them was obviously wrong.

Grinning, John stepped in and pulled a quarter from his jeans pocket. "Heads or tails?"

"Heads I win, tails you lose," Kyle said with a completely straight face.

Emily considered that for a second, then put her hands on her hips and glared at him in a perfect imitation of her mother. "Hey, that's not fair. I lose either way."

Grinning, he shrugged. "Can't blame a guy for trying."

After everyone stopped laughing, they both called heads, and John groaned. "Gimme a break, guys."

"Why don't they both do it?" Seth suggested while he adjusted a section of lights. "Take a picture, then let the other one put it on."

"That works," Ridge approved, grasping the star in one hand and lifting Emily with the other. "Ladies first."

After posing for Marianne's camera, Emily climbed down and carefully handed the ornament to Kyle. Ridge whispered something to him, then bro-hugged him with a proud smile. Kyle did the aw-shucks thing, but he was obviously pleased with whatever his stepfather had said. It was a nice moment, and Lisa noticed that Marianne sneaked in a shot of it before Kyle slid the star into place.

The warm exchange between Ridge and Kyle made her think of Seth and how he'd be with his own son someday. Fair and straightforward, but affectionate in the same masculine way Ridge and her brothers were. That was when it hit her.

Seth fit into her family perfectly. Like a puzzle piece in an open spot, Seth filled the empty place beside her very nicely, and she could easily imagine them together in the future.

But not now, she admitted with a sigh. Their paths were running parallel to one another, and they wouldn't cross for a while, if ever. Long before then, someone would catch his eye, and he'd adjust his plans to include her.

Watching him fiddle with some of the upper ornaments, Lisa couldn't keep back a wistful sigh. She wanted him to be happy, but she couldn't help wishing she was the one he'd make those concessions for. At least, she wouldn't mind giving it a try.

Seth Hansen was the kind of guy who made a girl rethink her priorities.

"Well, I've got a big day tomorrow, so I'd best be going," he said, circling the room with a grateful look. "Thanks so much for inviting me tonight. I had a great time."

Lisa smiled as Caty and the kids hugged him, and the guys lined up to shake his hand. Marianne sent Lisa one of her nudging looks, which Lisa pointedly ignored. Shaking her head, Marianne turned to their guest.

"You're welcome anytime, Seth," she said, embracing him. "Merry Christmas."

"To all of you, too," he answered, lifting his hand in farewell.

"I'll go with you," Lisa offered, taking her pink denim jacket from the rack by the door and slipping it on. She'd love it if he could stay longer, but she understood his desire to get a good night's sleep before his long drive.

Outside, her eyes went to the gnarled oak they all considered Ethan's tree. This was their third Christmas without him, but sometimes she missed him so much, her heart ached. With no direct memories of her mother, he was the only parent she'd ever known.

"Something wrong?"

The worry in Seth's voice brought her back to the present, and she turned to him with a sad smile. "Not really. Just thinking about my dad."

Seth's gaze went in the direction she'd been staring, then came back to her. "Is there something special about that tree?"

"It was Dad's favorite place on the whole farm. It's been here forever, and he and the boys used to eat lunch under there when they were working."

Seth smiled understanding. "I think lots of Sawyers did that in the past, too."

That he'd instinctively picked up on what she hadn't told him made her wonder. Was she doing the right thing letting him walk out of her life?

"So you're headed home in the morning," she said instead. This time, she was the one who couldn't meet his eyes.

"Yeah. Mom's making a big lunch, and it takes about three hours to get there. I've got a couple things to finish up, so I'll get started around nine."

"The diner will be hopping tomorrow." Lisa pulled a small package from her jacket pocket. "I should give you this now."

To her surprise, he frowned at the box wrapped in shiny gold paper. "I didn't get you anything. What an idiot. It's Christmas—I should've thought to get you a present."

"You tutored me so I won't make a fool of myself while I'm in Europe. You couldn't have bought me anything better than that."

Apparently satisfied, he opened her present. Inside, a heavy pewter key fob was pegged to a velvet board embossed with *Harland Jewelry*. Seth lifted it out and tilted it into the light coming from the kitchen windows to read the inscription. "Be strong and courageous."

"I had them engrave it special for you."

"Because I need to be strong and courageous?"

"Because you *are* strong and courageous." When his eyes met hers, she added, "I got it to thank you."

"For what?"

"For everything. Saving Pastor Charles, helping with the church and Cleo. For being my friend," she added with a heartfelt smile.

Taking the key chain out of the box, he hefted it in his hand. "This feels like it could take a real beating. I had one like it when I was younger."

"I got the idea from your mom. She said—"

His delighted expression dimmed considerably, and his eyes froze on her like icicles. "You talked to my mom?"

"Well, yes," Lisa stammered, suddenly terrified that she'd done something horribly wrong. In a desperate attempt to smooth it over, she went on in a rush. "I wanted to get you something you'd really like, and I figured she'd have some suggestions."

"You've never even met my parents." His deep voice was so measured it sent a chill creeping up her spine. "How did you get their number? Aunt Ruth?"

"I looked it up online, in the Fayetteville white pages."

"Unbelievable. You hunted down my parents."

"Not really." When he glared at her, she realized the difference was purely semantics. "Now that I see how angry you are, maybe it wasn't such a good plan."

"Angry? This is the kind of thing stalkers do."

"Don't be ridiculous," she shot back. "I wasn't stalking you, I was trying to buy you a gift."

"What else did she tell you? How pathetic I was after I lost that thing? How I thought losing it meant something awful was gonna happen? I was right, you know. A week later, my arm was in pieces and my best friend was dead."

She'd never seen him like this. Raging without reason, glaring at her as though she'd invaded his very private—very painful—life. If after all this time he could still think that about her, she didn't know how to change his mind.

She tried to snatch the box away from

him, but he held it out of reach. "You really don't get it, do you?"

"Not even a little. Why don't you straighten me out?"

Jaw clenched as if he was struggling to keep his temper, he glowered at her in a way she'd never seen from him. "I'm disgusted. Ever since I came home, you were the first person to treat me like I wasn't made of glass. Everyone else babies me, and I thought you were different. Turns out I was wrong."

He spat those last words as if they tasted bitter in his mouth. Since he did have a point, she probably should have backed off and apologized.

Instead, she drew herself up to her full height and looked him dead in the eyes. "Oh, get over yourself, Mr. High and Mighty. If someone trying to do something nice for you disgusts you, you're not the man I thought you were."

Too furious to stand there one more second, she spun on her heel and stalked away from him. She heard him mumble something nasty, then his truck door opened and slammed shut. As he drove around the circle, the sound of gravel spitting from under the tires had an angry quality to it. Only then did she look back.

She glimpsed his face, rigid and furious, as the truck flew past her and out toward the road. It was his own fault, she reasoned. Their evening didn't have to end this way. They should have had a nice, warm moment, maybe a goodbye kiss, before he left.

Stubborn beyond belief, she railed silently. Then again, maybe that was a good sign. The man currently racing away from her as fast as he could was very different from the one she'd met just after Thanksgiving. Seth was more personable now, and his newfound confidence would force people to stop treating him like a wounded little boy. Combine that with his stunning good looks, and he'd be irresistible to any female over twenty and breathing.

Sadly, Lisa knew that once he left Harland, she'd never see him again.

Chapter Twelve

The next morning, Seth was shoving things into his big duffel bag when his cell phone rang. Checking the caller ID, he grinned. "Hey, Mom."

"Merry Christmas Eve! Are you on your way?"

"Soon. I have to finish up a few things, but I should be on the road by nine."

"Then we'll see you for lunch."

"That depends," he teased as he zipped the bag closed. The clothes inside were clean, and he knew he'd have to convince her not to unpack and rewash them when he got home. "What're you having?"

"Your favorite," she said as though it

should have been obvious. "Roast beef and mashed potatoes."

"For lunch?" He groaned. "Why not just throw me on the couch and tell me to take a nap?"

"Your sense of humor's coming back," she commented with a laugh. "It's nice to hear it again."

Since he'd been a teenager, she'd complained nonstop about his slightly edgy wit. He had a feeling her approval wouldn't last. "We'll see what you think of it at New Year's."

"You sound more tired than when we talked yesterday morning. Is everything okay?"

The hesitance in her tone made him cringe. He wasn't even home yet, and she was walking on eggshells. Then again, considering what he'd put her through during his long recovery, he couldn't blame her for being extra careful.

"When I get there, you can ask me all the questions you want. Might not answer, but you can ask." Any about Lisa Sawyer, he definitely wasn't fielding.

"You're such a pain," she scolded with another laugh. "Drive carefully."

"I will."

There was a pause, and he waited for her to ask him to call her from his halfway point. That she worried so much about him made him more determined than ever to stand on his own. When the request never came, he decided to give her a break.

"Well, I'd best get moving. I'll call you from that truck stop in Franklin."

"Thank you, honey. I didn't want to ask."

"I know. See you soon."

He turned his phone off and stared at it for a few moments. He'd debated confronting her about talking to Lisa, then thought better of it. Mom wouldn't have done it if she thought it would upset him, and he didn't want to start out their family Christmas with an argument that would probably leave her in tears and him in the doghouse.

Sighing, he slung his bag over his shoulder. His tools were already in the truck, and a quick check showed him the room was empty. It was as if his visit had never happened, he mused as he headed into the hallway. On the landing, he paused and looked through the open doors into the four rooms he'd refurbished.

In those, he saw plenty of evidence that he'd been there.

The new oak floors shone in the early sunlight, and the freshly painted walls stood ready for the tenants moving in after the holidays. He'd done a good job, he thought with pride as he went downstairs. And this time, he was walking away with everything intact.

Most everything, he amended when he strolled into the kitchen. Over the swinging doors, he saw Lisa out in the dining room, looking as if she'd just sledded in from the North Pole. In a red dress and candy-cane apron, she was wearing a cute elf's hat studded in jingle bells. She stopped at a table occupied by four good-looking men dressed for the outdoors. As she moved around them to pour coffee, the bright sound of bells accompanied her.

"Morning, guys." She greeted them with one of her beautiful smiles. "Pancakes or waffles?"

"Both." Grinning up at her, one of them added, "Very cute. You should dress like that all the time."

Laughing, she tossed her head to make the bells ring. "I can't sneak up on anyone."

"But think of all the tips you'd get."

Feeling a little nauseous, Seth turned away and found his aunt tapping cinnamon sugar onto a batch of steaming twisty donuts. When he reached in to sneak one, she smacked his hand before looking up.

When she saw it was him, she said, "I'm sorry, honey, help yourself. I thought you were that new busboy. He's always trying to get stuff past me."

"He'll learn." After swallowing, he grinned. "You don't even have to chew these. They fall apart in your mouth."

"No higher praise for a pastry chef." Picking up a canvas sleeve, she attached a decorating tip and started filling it with icing. "Now, tell me if this is none of my business—"

"Lisa and I had a fight, but everything's fine."

That wasn't completely true, but he'd get over it, and so would she. If what he'd just seen was any indication, she'd already forgotten about it. And him.

Aunt Ruth assessed him with a long, suspicious look. "What makes you think that's what I was going to ask?"

"You have some kind of trouble radar, that's why."

"Well, I meant to ask if you needed a hand with whatever's left to do over at the church." Piping the icing onto a fresh coffee cake, she added, "It's interesting that your mind went straight to Lisa, though. What happened with you two?"

Seth had been asking himself that question all night and still didn't have a good answer. "Nothing, just like I told you a month ago. We're too different for it to be any other way. Sorry to break your match-making streak."

"Don't you get smart with me, young man." The fond twinkle in her eyes took some of the sting out of her scolding. "I don't encourage people to get together for my own sake. If it's not meant to be, it's not meant to be. It's not like I'm keeping score."

"Good to know."

When he grinned at her, she huffed, "You're impossible. Get out of my kitchen."

"Yes, ma'am. We'll see you at Mom's New Year's party, right?"

"I wouldn't miss it."

She tilted her head in a silent command, and he dutifully kissed her cheek. Impulsively, he lifted her up and spun her around in a quick hug before setting her down.

Laughing, she demanded, "You almost gave me a heart attack! What was that for?"

"Everything. Merry Christmas, Auntie."

Emotion sparkled in her eyes, and she patted his shoulder with a sugar-coated hand. "Merry Christmas, Sethy. Have a good trip."

She embraced him again, and on that warm, fuzzy note he headed out. Crossing the street, he saw Gus was already at the church site, sitting on the tailgate of his antique truck. As Seth had asked, he'd parked out of sight behind the building.

Sipping coffee from a large Ruthy's Place to-go cup, Gus greeted him with a nod. "Morning."

"Morning. Thanks for helping me out." Looking into the bed, he smiled. "Nice tree."

"It's the biggest one they had at the nursery. You sure I can't help you pay for it?"

"No, I want to do this myself. Harland's been good to me," he added with heartfelt gratitude. "I want to leave something for the town."

"Then we'd best get to it." Reaching in, Gus took out two shovels and handed one to Seth. "Being a soldier and all, I'd imagine you know what to do with this."

While they dug, Seth realized that Gus's reference to his history had sailed by smoothly. He'd felt none of the tension or anxiety he'd reluctantly come to accept as the norm for him. He searched his brain for that old seizing-up feeling he used to get when his military past came up in conversation, but it was gone.

Glancing over at the little white church he'd helped to repair, he couldn't help wondering if Lisa was right. Had God brought him to Harland because this was where he would heal? For all the hard work and aggravation his visit had caused him, had the church project actually been a blessing in disguise?

Maybe, Seth mused, Jim Canfield's turnaround wasn't the only Christmas miracle that had happened in this small town.

"That oughta do it," Gus declared.

From his amused expression, Seth knew the old Marine had been waiting for him to come out of his fog. Since Gus wasn't calling him on it, Seth decided to let it be. He wasn't sure what his convoluted train of thought meant, and he wasn't keen on exploring it just now.

Gus backed his truck to the edge of the

hole they'd dug, and they tipped the tree into place. After heaping the dirt back in, they packed it down and stood back to admire their work.

Even though this was the best he could do, Seth frowned. "Doesn't quite measure up to the old one, does it?"

"Ten years or so, it will." Gus clapped a hand on his shoulder. "Nothing worth having comes easy, son. You have to be patient."

As usual, Seth got the feeling there was a deeper lesson in the wise words. Smiling his appreciation, he held out his hand. "It was an honor working with you, sir."

"Back at ya, son. Anytime you're looking for a change of scenery, you're welcome at my place. I've always got a use for someone who's as good with their hands as you are."

Not sure he'd heard that right, Seth cocked his head. "Are you offering me a job?"

"Sure am." He held up his hands in a calming gesture. "No pressure or anything, just an opportunity if you want it. What you do with it is up to you."

It was the first time anyone had had enough confidence in him to mention hiring him permanently, and Seth's heart soared knowing Gus had that much faith in him. He wasn't sure how to express that without getting all gushy, so he settled for a simple, "Thanks."

"Don't mention it. By the way," he muttered, glancing around. "I'm taking your aunt to the Christmas Eve service tonight. Officially."

"Really?" He couldn't help grinning at the excited twinkle in Gus's eyes. "Good for you."

"Don't know where we'll end up, but even if it's right where we are now, I figured it's time to give it a shot."

"Uncle Paul would've liked that," Seth approved. "If Aunt Ruth was gonna be with anyone else, I think he'd be happy it was you."

"I appreciate you saying that," Gus said in a gruff voice. "Paul and I were best friends our whole lives, so that means a lot to me."

"Merry Christmas."

"Merry Christmas to you, too."

Patting Seth's shoulder again, Gus climbed into his truck and pulled away from the church. When he was alone, Seth went up the back steps into the chapel.

On the altar, the pastor's lectern glowed under its new coat of varnish. Above it, the stained-glass window was still behind its protective casing. Climbing up on a ladder, Seth carefully removed the box he'd built and carried it down to store it in back. If they ever did major work on the church, it would come in handy.

With a cloth and some watered-down cleaner, he carefully wiped the dust from the artwork and put the ladder away. Standing in the aisle, he admired the sunlight streaming through the multicolored glass. It threw bits of color onto the new pews, accenting the carvings and color he and Lisa had so painstakingly matched to the old.

They'd made a good team, he thought with a frown. Beyond that, she'd found things in him that he'd thought were lost forever. Confidence, warmth, happiness.

From her kind and generous heart, she'd given him the most precious gift he could imagine.

She'd given him back himself.

She'd stepped over a very personal line calling Mom that way, but he hadn't taken it well, either. Their tiff wasn't entirely Lisa's fault, he realized now. Maybe he should have just sucked it up and swallowed his frustration the way he usually did.

No, that wouldn't have been right, either. And furious as she might be with him, he suspected Lisa would tell him the same. His impression that first day turned out to be accurate: she was a handful. More than he could manage right now, maybe ever. Grudgingly, he admitted that was one of the things he liked most about her.

She wasn't afraid to be exactly who she was. That was the most valuable lesson she'd taught him, and he had no intention of setting it aside just to make his life easier. Sliding his hand into his front pocket, he fingered the key chain she'd given him.

He'd known plenty of brave men and

women, soldiers who put aside their fear and did what had to be done. In her own way, Lisa was one of the strongest, most courageous people he'd ever met.

As that thought floated through his mind, a particularly bright shaft of sunlight burst through the altar window, making Jesus look as if He might come to life and step out of the frame. That unsettling feeling came over Seth the way it had the last time he saw that window, as if someone were trying to tell him something.

A month ago, he would have dismissed the concept as slightly insane, but now he recognized it for what it was. Gratitude. Busy as He must be with crises all over the world, God was thanking Seth for helping to restore this tiny North Carolina church in time to celebrate His son's birth.

Feeling his heart open to the faith he'd abandoned years ago, Seth smiled. "You're welcome."

When he heard one of the main doors creak open, he turned to find Pastor Charles framed in the doorway. Dressed in his usual gray suit, today he was wearing a red-and-green polka-dot version of his customary bow tie. As he strolled down the aisle, his head swept back and forth slowly and he smiled in approval.

"You like it?" Seth asked.

"It's more than beautiful," he replied softly. "It's a Christmas miracle."

Seth couldn't keep back a grin. "Yeah, I was just thinking the same thing. All those people, busy as they were, working together to make this happen. That's pretty impressive."

"It certainly is," the pastor said, taking a seat in one of the new pews. Running a hand over the back, he twisted to look behind him and then across the aisle. "They look exactly the same as the old ones." He swiveled to look at Seth with an I-told-you-so twinkle in his eyes. "I knew you could do it."

He hadn't done it alone, and Seth felt compelled to share the credit. "Lisa helped with that, matching the old stain so the new finish would be the same on all the wood."

Chuckling, the fatherly man cocked his head in mild scolding. "Do you even know how to take a compliment, son?"

"Not really. Not used to them, I guess."

"Praise comes rarely to some of us," Pastor Charles said gently. "When it's offered honestly, we should learn to accept it."

"I'll work on that."

Suddenly, Seth felt himself tensing up, as if he'd hung around just a little too long. He hadn't meant for anyone to find him in the church, and despite all his efforts, his old habits hadn't quite died out yet.

"Well, I'd best be going," he said, offering his hand to the preacher. "Thanks again for everything."

The man stood and held his arms open. After hesitating, Seth decided it would be rude to refuse the gesture. He stepped into the hug, stiffly returning it.

As if sensing Seth's discomfort, Pastor Charles quickly pulled away and beamed up at him. "You'll always be welcome in this house, Seth. We'll be here whenever you decide to come back."

"We, meaning you and God?"

"Yes, and Harland, too." Sweeping a hand through the air, he added, "You've worked your way into their hearts, and they'd be happy to make you one of them. If that's what you want."

The backpedaling comment made Seth laugh. "You learned that from your kids, didn't you?"

"I've found that when you force-feed things to people, they tend to fling them back at you."

"Like strained peas?"

Smiling, the man nodded. "But if you offer them something they want and invite them to the table, eventually they'll sit down and help themselves."

"You're really good with those religious metaphors, aren't you?"

He met Seth's teasing with a good-natured grin. "Just because it's a metaphor doesn't mean it's not true. Wrapping a lesson in a story goes back a lot farther than I do."

"Got me there," Seth allowed with a grin of his own. "Merry Christmas, sir."

"And to you, Seth. May God bless you and your family."

During his long drive to Fayetteville, Seth could only think about one thing.

Lisa.

She kept creeping into his thoughts, and he'd push her away, only to have her pop in again. He'd pass a car full of kids and think about last night at the Sawyer farm, sharing those family moments with her. When he glanced over at the clock on the dashboard, the pewter key chain she'd given him glowed warmly in the sunlight.

When "All I Want for Christmas Is You" came on the radio, he decided fate was out to get him. He had a feeling that from now on, whenever he heard that song, he'd think of the day he met her and their first kiss under the mistletoe at the diner. No doubt, Aunt Ruth would tuck that photo away and look at it in the future, shaking her head over what might have been.

That thought brought up another one that shocked him. He could have had everything he'd ever wanted, if he'd just been smart enough to reach out and grab what Lisa had offered him. *Stupid, stubborn pride,* he groaned silently. Not long ago, he would have skulked away with his head down because he didn't know how to remedy his mistake. The man he was now simply couldn't leave things the way they were.

After Christmas, he'd go back to Harland and apologize to Lisa the way he should have this morning. It might not get him a mushy happily-ever-after ending, but at least they could break even as friends. He owed her that much.

By his halfway mark, it dawned on Seth that it wasn't just Lisa calling him back to Harland. It was the town itself, the folks who lived there who'd opened their hearts to a disillusioned soldier and made him feel welcome. People who saw him hurting and went out of their way to help him recover what he'd lost.

And it was the church. Battered and broken but still standing, it reminded him of himself when he'd first arrived. Struggling to stand, needing to be shored up until it could be brought back to what it used to be. The pastor had gotten to him, he thought with a grin. Offering him something he wanted so he'd come back. Sneaky.

Which brought him back to Lisa. Before their fight, he'd seen the wistful look in her eyes. Despite his best efforts, she'd gotten attached to him. If he apologized and she forgave him, what would he do next? Move to Harland, work for Gus and date Lisa? Chances were it wouldn't take him long to completely fall in love with her. What then?

That path was a huge leap from where he was now. Maybe if he turned the problem over in his mind for a while, the answer would jump out at him the way it did when he was working his way through a difficult carpentry project.

The only difference was, Lisa wasn't a block of wood or something out of his tool-box. She was a sweet, sensitive woman who saw something in him no other woman ever had. For some crazy reason, she'd deemed him worth the effort it had taken her to break through his defenses and drag him back into the world.

The big question was, should he do something about it or let her go?

Sighing, he pulled into the truck stop and called his mother as he'd promised. The excitement in her voice earlier was nothing compared to what he heard now, and he grinned as he clicked his phone off and pulled back onto the highway.

He still wasn't sure what he'd be doing in the New Year, but today he was going home. It felt good.

That afternoon, Seth went outside with his father to help him bring in the tree. After the huge lunch Mom had made, he figured the activity would do him good.

"You know this thing won't fit in the living room, right?" Seth asked.

Stepping back from the enormous Douglas fir, Dad cocked his head one way and then the other. "This is the one your mother wanted."

Seth got the message loud and clear. She'd been through so much worrying over him, she deserved whatever tree she wanted. He didn't bother to ask how much it had cost, because he knew it really didn't matter. She didn't often ask for anything and when she did, Dad made it happen.

That was love, Seth realized with sudden clarity. Doing everything in your power to make someone else's dreams come true.

While they trimmed the tree down to size, Dad asked about the rehabbing Seth had done for Aunt Ruth and at the church. Seth answered the questions, but he was only half listening. After a while, his father set down the saw and looked at him over the waist-high stack of excess pine boughs.

"You're not saying much. Something on your mind, son?"

Trying to avoid worrying him, Seth hedged, "Mom's roast beef always knocks me out."

"That's not going to work with me," Dad

warned him. "If you don't want to talk, that's fine, but I can see something's bothering you."

"It's nothing, honest. I've just been really busy, and I'm still tired, I guess."

That was the wrong thing to say, he realized instantly. Concern flooded Dad's eyes, and Seth quickly amended, "Not the bad kind of tired. The kind you get when you're done with a big job you're really happy with."

His worried expression relaxed a bit, and he chuckled. "Who is she?"

"Who?"

"I know that look, Seth. When I first met your mom, I looked a lot like you do right now." Balancing the bow saw on the chopping block, he rested his hands across the top. "Who is she?"

Busted, Seth thought, giving in to the grin that seemed to keep popping up when he thought about going back to see Lisa. He had no doubt she'd give him some grief at first, but they'd work it out somehow. He was determined not to surrender just yet.

"Her name's Lisa Sawyer. She works for Aunt Ruth at the diner, but she's an amazing artist. You should see the way she paints."

"Is this the girl who called to ask for advice on a present?"

"Yeah," Seth replied with a sigh. "We got in a fight over it, which was totally my fault, so she's pretty mad at me."

"You're going to apologize, then."

It wasn't a question, and Seth nodded contritely. "Yes, sir. Right after Christmas."

"Tell me about her."

As Seth described all they'd done together, his father listened without interrupting. When he was finished, Dad said, "She sounds pretty special."

"She is," Seth admitted without a second thought. "I've never met anyone like her."

"Really? Then let me ask you something."

"Sure."

"What in the world are you doing here?"

Chapter Thirteen

"Would you look at that?" John asked when they stepped out of their cars near the church that evening. Pointing to a spotlighted oak tree, he asked, "Who planted that?"

People were bypassing the steps to go check it out, and the Sawyers joined the procession out of curiosity. There was no note, only a care tag attached to the trunk of a sturdy tree that was listed as three years old. Not a sapling that would keel over in a moderate wind, Lisa noticed. Something strong and capable of weathering a storm without breaking.

Like Seth.

He'd been so interested in the old Sawyer family picture, her finely tuned intuition told her he'd been the one to think of replacing the tree. Running a hand through the bare branches, she recalled telling him how much it meant to her, back when they'd hardly known anything about each other.

He'd remembered, she realized as a wave of regret washed over her. Remembered and made it right. It was just like him to do something generous like this without taking credit for it. During the day, her anger toward him had faded, and she wished he was here to see how much his anonymous gift meant to the town.

Turning away, she followed her family into the church. There were a few details still to finish up, but after its brush with disaster, the little white church looked more beautiful to her than ever. Two Christmas trees twined with natural garlands and tiny white lights flanked the famous window, and garlands were draped everywhere.

The hurricane lamps in the windows added their own glow, and the conversation buzzing through the sanctuary had a warm, melodic ring to it. After being empty during construction, it was nice to see the place full of people, the way it was meant to be.

That made her think of Seth again, and she wished things had ended better between them. She still didn't think she'd done anything wrong, but it would have been nice to send him off with a cheerful "Merry Christmas," rather than memories of them glaring at each other.

She slid down her family's usual pew so she could get a full view of the decorations. Once the family was settled, she made space for a couple more people at her end. Judging by the number of folks coming in the door, they'd need every available spot.

Absorbed in a conversation with the Millers, she paid no attention when someone sat down beside her. When whoever it was reached into the rack on the back of the pew in front of them for a hymnal, she caught a glimpse of their hand. Covered in scars and brown stain, it was a very familiar hand.

Hardly daring to believe her own eyes, she slowly angled her head to confirm what she already knew.

Seth grinned back at her. "Merry Christmas Eve."

Lisa opened her mouth, but nothing came out. That was slightly ridiculous, because a zillion questions were bouncing around in her head. One popped to the surface, and she stammered, "What are you doing here?"

"Trying to find the right hymn." Squinting at the sign listing tonight's songs, he asked, "Is that a 3 or an 8?"

Astounding as it was that he was in church for anything other than repair work, she focused on the more pressing question. "I mean, what are you doing here in Harland? I thought you were spending Christmas at home."

Reaching over, he took her hand and brushed a kiss over the back. As his eyes locked with hers, they shifted to a color she couldn't have mixed on her palette if she tried for a month. A pale sky blue, they held none of the iciness she'd seen there just before she stalked away from him. Tonight, they glimmered with a warmth she could almost feel.

"I'm going back in the morning," he explained. "But I wanted to be here tonight, to see how everything looks."

She could tell he wanted to say something else, and in the spirit of the season, she decided to give him a break. Reaching over, she squeezed his hand. "It's okay, Seth. I'm sorry, too."

"I'm not usually such a jerk, honest."

"I know."

"You didn't do anything wrong, and I completely lost my mind."

Trying not to laugh, she smiled instead. "I know that, too."

"I'm really, really sorry." Grimacing, he leaned closer and murmured, "Can you forgive me?"

"Since it's you, yes." Giving him a mock

frown, she pointed at him. "But don't do it again."

"Yes, your highness."

They both laughed, and she gave him a quick hug. When the organist started playing, they stood to sing the opening of "Hark the Herald Angels Sing," but Lisa couldn't stop smiling.

Seth had come back. She didn't know why exactly, and he'd be leaving tomorrow, but she didn't much care. Having him here, grinning down at her while they sang, was the greatest Christmas gift ever.

Once the last strains of organ music died away, Pastor Charles stood in front of his restored lectern and held his arms open as if he were embracing them all at once.

"Merry Christmas to you all." They answered him, and he sent a grateful smile around the crowd. "We're gathered here in this place on this blessed night only because so many people volunteered their time, energy and a good amount of money to make it happen. It may be slightly unusual, but I'd like you all to give yourselves a hand. You've earned it."

Beaming at them, he applauded, and everyone followed his example. Even the Scroogey Jim Canfield, Lisa noticed with surprise. She hoped his recent change of heart would carry into the New Year.

"And to whoever planted our new tree," the pastor continued, "thank you. While I respect your desire to remain anonymous, I'd like you to know that your generous gift has touched all of our hearts and will continue doing so for years to come."

With that, he launched into an uplifting sermon about the birth of a baby who would grow into a man offering His followers the most precious gift of all: salvation. Walking in His footsteps, the pastor reminded them, was the path to having a good life on Earth and eternal peace in Heaven.

His words were the perfect segue to their closing hymn, and everyone belted out "Joy to the World" with more enthusiasm than skill. To Lisa's ears, the sound was even more glorious because they'd come so close to celebrating Christmas packed into the dining room at Ruthy's Place.

Chancing a look up at Seth, she caught him smiling at her and easily smiled back. Leaning against him, she started the second verse, wishing this completely perfect night would never end.

When the service was over, the Sawyers raced back to the farm to put the last-minute touches on their annual Christmas Eve party. John peeled out of the lot in his classic Triumph, beating them all home by a good two minutes. Knowing how sore a winner he was, Lisa prepared a few zingers for when he tried to rub their noses in it.

This year, she'd strung lit garland around the sign marking their lane, and she was glad to see the solar-powered lights were still nice and bright. As Seth drove down the long driveway, he let out a low whistle. "The place looks like a Norman Rockwell painting."

She laughed. "We Sawyers do everything big."

"Yeah, but this is something else."

He parked next to the barn, out of the way near the Sawyers' own cars. That he'd thought to leave space for their guests was so considerate, she impulsively hugged his arm.

Angling a look at her, he asked, "What's that for?"

"For being here." Afraid that might sound clingy or girlfriend-ish, she hastily added, "I know it's a long drive, and it was really nice of you to come all this way."

"I wanted to be here." Turning to face her, he gently took her hand. "I wanted to be with you."

Lisa's heart soared at the tenderness running through his voice. She'd heard things like that plenty of times, from more guys than she cared to recall. But none of them meant those words the way Seth did. Before she could think of something to say, he leaned in and kissed her.

"I love you, Lisa."

Shocked to her toes, she yanked back with a gasp that made her choke. While she tried to stop coughing, poor Seth sat there looking mortified. And regretful. As she struggled to regain her composure, she patted his shoulder, trying to ease his mind until she could say something.

"I'm sorry," she croaked. "I didn't mean to react like that."

"It's okay."

As he drew back, she reached out and grasped his shoulders to keep him close. After a kiss to soothe his embarrassment, she said, "I love you, too. I just never dreamed you'd feel the same way about me. You really caught me by surprise with that one."

"Imagine how I felt when it first hit me." His wry look was tinged with a warmth she felt all the way to her toes. "I'm not good with this mushy stuff."

"Men never are. That's why God made women the way we are, to teach guys how to be mushy."

"Ya think?"

"Definitely. If Matt and Ridge can learn, so can you."

"So this time you'll teach me." Seth gave

her that knee-weakening grin she'd assumed she would never see again. "I like the sound of that."

For the first time in his life, Seth understood the phrase "walking on air." With his arm around Lisa, he strolled toward the old farmhouse feeling as though nothing could ever beat him again. The most remarkable woman he'd ever met loved him, and before long they'd be spending every single day together, preparing for their trip. Practicing languages, planning day trips, arguing over which landmarks to see first.

He couldn't wait.

Tonight would have been perfect enough on its own, he thought with a grin, but it was just the beginning. As he and Lisa paused on the back porch to greet some of the other guests, he saw there wasn't enough room for everyone inside. Smaller versions of the huge tree stood on both porches, strung with lights and simple red-and-green balls. Like the sign, the railings were draped in Lisa's trademark lit garlands. Christmas music poured from John's mega-stereo, and Seth counted twelve speakers hanging from the porch posts.

When Lisa was finished chatting with her friends, Seth pulled the door open for her.

"Tucker, no!"

Out of reflex, Seth slammed the door closed and stepped in front of it just as Tucker came barreling in from the barn. Fortunately, he was able to stop the determined Lab or he'd have smashed face-first into the glass.

John came jogging up behind the crazy dog, laughing and panting at the same time. "Nice one, Seth. I was getting some ice from the freezer in the barn, and he blew right past me. If he managed to get in the house, he'd tear that buffet apart in two seconds. Marianne'd never let me hear the end of it."

"Glad to help."

"I'll trade you," John replied, hefting the two bags of ice he was carrying. After they'd made the switch, he grinned at his sister. "This guy fits right in around here, doesn't he?"

Beaming up at Seth, she circled her hands around his arm. "He sure does."

"Come on, you." Bending over, John tugged on Tucker's collar. "We'd best get you locked back down before Marianne sees you."

After John had taken the dog around the corner of the barn, Seth decided it was safe to open the door again.

Everywhere he looked people were gathered in groups, talking and laughing while they ate their way through a buffet that held four hams, a carving board full of roast beef, several varieties of rolls and every kind of salad he'd ever seen. On a side table, a collection of cakes and pies were clustered around a mountain of Christmas cookies.

All that food made him think of Aunt Ruth, and he remembered that Gus had mentioned bringing her to the service tonight. Wondering if they were here, Seth scoped the crowd and found them talking to some people, Gus's arm resting lightly over her shoulders. Maybe, Seth thought with a grin, his aunt was right about that Christmas magic, after all.

"Lisa!"

They both turned at the sound of Marianne's excited voice. With Ridge in tow, she pushed her way through the crowd and hugged them both. Something told Seth there was more to the gleam in her eyes than holiday spirit.

"I wanted to tell you before, but it was too crazy at the church." Pausing, she took a deep breath and hurried on. "Guess why I'm so sick all the time."

"Because you're pregnant?" Lisa guessed.

"With twins," Ridge filled in, hugging Marianne closer. "We just found out today."

"Twins," Lisa echoed, embracing Ridge and then her sister. Holding Marianne at arm's length, she added, "We really need to start shopping for baby clothes."

"I can't believe it," Marianne continued. "It's just incredible."

Some of the joy had left Lisa's face, and

she got serious. "You're going to need some help."

"Don't even think about that. You're going to Europe, and I'll be fine. It's not a problem. Ridge and the boys are here all the time, and Caty will be around."

"But Caty will have her own baby to take care of, and the farm keeps the guys so busy." Marianne opened her mouth to protest, but Lisa cut her off. "Before you mention Kyle and Emily, they're just kids."

"You don't know anything about babies, either."

"No, but I can clean and do laundry and cook. Kind of."

After a moment, they all broke out laughing.

"Okay," Lisa relented good-naturedly, "point taken. But you *are* going to need some help around here. Do you have any other ideas?"

"We'll hire a housekeeper," Ridge suggested. "Folks do it all the time, so it shouldn't be too hard."

"Someone who'd be good with the kids?" Lisa scoffed. "Isn't that a nanny?"

"A housekeeper-slash-nanny, then," he amended casually.

Lisa laughed again. "Good luck finding someone who can keep this house up to Marianne's standards."

"We've got time to be picky," Marianne declared. "We probably won't need anyone until summer, and there will be lots of girls home from college, looking for work. I'll find the right person somewhere."

While they debated various girls they knew around town, it struck Seth that he'd been part of what should have been a strictly family moment. That the Sawyers considered him part of their close-knit group touched him deeply, and his mind returned to the epiphany he'd had earlier.

He belonged with Lisa, wherever she was. Harland or Helsinki, it didn't matter to him. As long as they were together, he'd be the happiest man on earth. When Marianne and Ridge moved on to spread their happy news, Seth gently tugged Lisa toward the mistletoe.

Looking up at it, she grinned at him. "You know, this is where Matt proposed to Caty."

"Under the mistletoe?" When she nodded, he chuckled. "I told you, it makes people do crazy things."

After a long kiss, he settled his arms around her and smiled down at her. "I love you, Lisa."

Reaching up, she rested her hand on his cheek and stood on tiptoe to kiss him. "I love you, too."

"Y'know, this is what I've always wanted for Christmas."

That got him one of her bright, breezy laughs that always made him feel incredible. "A girl?"

"Not just any girl," he corrected, rubbing noses with her. "*The* girl."

"Meaning me?"

"Meaning you."

"Then I guess it's a good thing you decided to come to Harland, seeing as that's where I was."

"Yes, it was." Gazing down at her, he smiled and rested his forehead against hers. "A very good thing."

Epilogue

Paris in April was the most beautiful place Lisa had ever seen.

Of course, the fact that she and Seth were on their honeymoon definitely enhanced the experience. In Rome, they'd explored the Colosseum, Saint Peter's Square and more stunning cathedrals than she could keep track of. In London, they'd strolled through neighborhoods people had been living in since long before Harland even existed. The only tour she refused to take was the one that went to the Tower Bridge. Knowing its bloody history gave her the creeps, and she had no intention of going anywhere near its haunted walls.

Buckingham Palace and the museums were awe-inspiring, and she dragged Seth through one charming park after another, snapping photos while she drank in the green beauty of the English gardens and perfectly groomed hedges.

A quick train ride had brought them to Paris, and she was officially in love. Cobblestones bore the names of famous artists who'd strolled along the same walkways centuries ago, and she wondered if they'd been as dazzled by the city as she was.

Now it was almost sunset, and she was sitting on a bench, staring at the Eiffel Tower as the nighttime lights began to come on.

It was even better than her poster, she thought with a dreamy little sigh.

"That sounds good," her husband commented as he joined her with a cup in each hand. He offered her one, cautioning, "I had the waitress add extra sugar for you, so be careful."

Lisa took a cautious sip and closed her eyes with another sigh. "Perfect."

"Glad to hear that." After swallowing

some of his, Seth leaned back and stretched his arms across the back of the bench. "How're you doing with the jet lag?"

Cuddling against his chest, she replied, "Better. I look less like I just crawled out of those underground crypts in Rome."

He dropped a kiss on top of her head. "I never did think you looked like that. Not even our first day in Venice when you tripped getting out of the gondola and almost went into the canal."

"I was so tired, I had no idea the dock was that far away." Since she hadn't ended up in the filthy water, she could laugh at the memory. "It's a good thing you were there to catch me."

"I'd never let you fall. Besides, your family made me promise to bring you back in one piece."

She giggled. "Yeah, that sounds like them. I think we're supposed to do some mountain climbing in Austria, so you'd better hang on tight that day."

"No problem there."

Seth reached down and took her hand in

his, giving it a reassuring squeeze. While she'd never have considered making that climb on her own, with him there she felt bold enough to give it a try. Whatever problems they might have had in the past, she'd never doubted that this remarkably strong, capable man would do everything in his power to keep her safe.

That he'd insisted on marrying her just made him more amazing.

"I talked to Marianne today," she said. "Their phone's been ringing off the hook with calls for you. Apparently, anytime a customer even hints at doing renovations, Gus gives them your name. Since they know we're away, they call the farm."

"No doubt, some of them are after my interior designer," he commented, grinning over at her. "Aunt Ruth told me her new tenants all gush about how nice their rooms are. One girl broke down and cried when she saw hers. Said she's never had her own room, much less one that looks like it came out of a design magazine."

"We make a good team. You do the hard stuff, I do the packaging."

"Yeah." Giving her an appreciative male look, he added a lazy kiss. "I sure do like your packaging."

While they sat in companionable silence, the sun slipped down behind the tower, lighting the open-worked structure in a fantastic array of red, orange and yellow, with a tinge of pink floating around the edges. As the lights lining the girders grew steadily brighter, it was an incredible sight.

"C'est incroyable," she breathed, trotting out one of the French phrases he'd taught her all those months ago in her living room.

"Yeah, it is."

Surprised by the conviction in his voice, she angled a look up at him. "You really think so? I mean, you've seen it before."

"I've seen all these places before." Snugging her closer with his arm, he rested his cheek in her hair. "But they look different now that I'm seeing them with you. It's all new for you, and that makes it fun for me. Besides, if I didn't know more Italian than you, you'd have had sheep's tongue for breakfast the other day."

"Oh, don't remind me!" Lisa laughed. "I was so embarrassed, I ended up ordering toast and jam."

"I'm telling you, you can never go wrong with *'Excusi, signora,* do you speak English?'"

"I'm much better with French," she reminded him curtly.

"Let's hope so."

He laughed, and she decided she'd had enough razzing for a while. "Shut up and watch the sunset."

"Yes, ma'am."

After several minutes, she felt him shift as if he was uncomfortable and glanced up at him. "You okay?"

Giving her the kind of hesitant look she hadn't seen in months, he asked, "Can I tell you something?"

Turning, she gave him her full attention. "Sure. It sounds important."

"It is."

Trying not to invent things that could be

wrong, Lisa cautioned herself to be patient with him. During the past few months he'd been in Harland working for Gus, she'd learned that Seth came to things in his own way, at his own speed. It was part of what made him Seth, the man she loved enough to give up some of her treasured independence to become his wife. She wouldn't change him for anything in the world.

When he swiveled from the bench and went down on his knee in front of her, she was really glad she'd waited.

Taking the hand that sparkled with the rings he'd given her, he looked up at her with pure, honest emotion flooding his eyes. "Lisa, I know it was a big leap for you to marry a guy like me. I promise I'll do my best to make sure you don't regret taking that chance."

Lisa's mind drifted back to her conversation with Marianne about finding the right guy for her. Seth was the knight in shining armor she'd been searching for all that time, and she thanked God for sending him to her.

Reaching out, she framed his face in her hands and said, "Seth, your past doesn't matter to me, only what we have right now. You're everything I've ever wanted."

"I just hope you always feel that way."

Smiling, she leaned in and answered him with a kiss.

* * * * *

If you enjoyed Mia Ross's story,
be sure to check out the other books
this month from Love Inspired!

Dear Reader,

I just love Christmas. With any luck at all, that showed in this story. Gathering family together, laughing and catching up are my favorite parts of the holidays. The Sawyers' Christmas traditions reflect the ones my family and I enjoy, year after year. They're some of the things I want my kids to remember when they have their own families someday.

Thank you for taking time out of your hectic holiday schedule to visit Harland for a little while. If you'd like to send me a message, you'll find me online at Facebook, Twitter and at www.miaross.com. While you're there, send me a message in your favorite format. I'd love to hear from you!

Merry Christmas!
Mia Ross

Questions for Discussion

1. Lisa is attracted to Seth from the first time she sees him, but she resists it because he's obviously troubled. When she decides to give him a chance, she's glad she changed her mind. Do you think she made the right decision?

2. Even though Lisa quickly realizes Seth is a special guy, she's determined not to get involved with him because she fears losing her independence. Have you ever pushed away an opportunity because it didn't fit into your plans?

3. Christmas is a special time for family, but Seth feels disconnected from people in general. Although he's not from Harland, he develops a special connection to the church he's fixing. Has something like this ever happened to you?

4. Seth has a problem with roofing contractor Jim Canfield from the start.

Eventually, they find common ground and learn to respect each other. Can you think of a time when you were able to make a similar concession to someone else? How did it work out?

5. As the youngest in her family, Lisa is always trying to assert her independence and do her own thing. Do you think birth order can really shape someone's personality, or are people born a certain way?

6. Even though he's hesitant to get serious with Lisa, Seth urges Gus to pursue a relationship with Ruthy. Do you know someone who gives advice easily but doesn't follow it themselves?

7. Seth's military background gives him a definite edge in a crisis, but it also makes him wary. If you know a current or former soldier, do you see the same quality in their behavior?

8. PTSD is a term most people are familiar with these days. While we know more

about its causes, the best approaches for helping someone recover are still evolving. Do you know someone struggling with it? If so, can you think of ways people around them could help?

9. Ruthy is a notorious matchmaker, and at first Lisa and Seth resent her meddling. Later, they realize she was right in pushing them together. Do you think people should interfere when their heart is in the right place, or should they let others work things out for themselves?

10. Somehow, the church's antique stained-glass window survives the storm that damages so much of the building. This small miracle begins Seth's path back to his faith. Can you think of other occurrences like this that defy logical explanation?

11. When Marianne reveals she's expecting twins, Lisa considers delaying her trip to stay in Harland and help her sister. Until that point in the story, she's

determined to go to Europe, no matter what. What do you think changed in Lisa along the way?

12. Although she enjoys all the cities they tour, Lisa's favorite is Paris. What is your favorite place to visit? Why?

REQUEST YOUR FREE BOOKS!

2 FREE INSPIRATIONAL NOVELS IN TRUE LARGE PRINT
PLUS 2 FREE MYSTERY GIFTS

Love Inspired™

TRUE LARGE PRINT

YES! Please send me 2 FREE Love Inspired® True Large Print novels and my 2 FREE mystery gifts (gifts are worth about $10). After receiving them, if I don't wish to receive any more books, I can return the shipping statement marked "cancel". If I don't cancel, I will receive 3 brand-new true large print novels every month and be billed just $7.99 per book in the U.S. or $9.99 per book in Canada. That's a savings of at least 33% off the cover price. It's quite a bargain! Shipping and handling is just 50¢ per book in the U.S. and 75¢ per book in Canada.* I understand that accepting the 2 free books and gifts places me under no obligation to buy anything. I can always return the shipment and cancel at any time. Even if I never buy another book, the two free books and gifts are mine to keep forever.

117/307 IDN FV74

Name _____ (PLEASE PRINT)

Address _____ Apt. #

City _____ State/Prov. _____ Zip/Postal Code

Signature (if under 18, a parent or guardian must sign)

Mail to the **Reader Service:**
IN U.S.A.: P.O. Box 1867, Buffalo, NY 14240-1867
IN CANADA: P.O. Box 609, Fort Erie, Ontario L2A 5X3

* Terms and prices subject to change without notice. Prices do not include applicable taxes. Sales tax applicable in N.Y. Canadian residents will be charged applicable taxes. Offer not valid in Quebec. This offer is limited to one order per household. Not valid for current subscribers to Love Inspired True Large Print books. All orders subject to credit approval. Credit or debit balances in a customer's account(s) may be offset by any other outstanding balance owed by or to the customer. Please allow 4 to 6 weeks for deliver. Offer available while quantities last.

Your Privacy—The Reader Service is committed to protecting your privacy. Our Privacy Policy is available online at www.ReaderService.com or upon request from the Reader Service.

We make a portion of our mailing list available to reputable third parties that offer products we believe may interest you. If you prefer that we not exchange your name with third parties, or if you wish to clarify or modify your communication preferences, please visit us at www.ReaderService.com/consumerschoice or write to us at Reader Service Preference Service, P.O. Box 9062, Buffalo, NY 14269. Include your complete name and address.

LITLP12TR